The Communicator
The Saga of Bo and Shana

DOUGLAS GREEN

ISBN: 145055363X
ISBN-13: 9781450553636
Library of Congress Control Number: 2010901249

Contents

Introduction

A small Indian village reservation located in North Dakota encounters a falling meteorite on a normal summer night. The meteor lands in the Cayman River near their village. The villagers notice the meteor passing overhead across the sky. They never hear the meteor land, so they ignore it and continue on with their evening activities. The meteor lands about fifty miles away from the Indian reservation in the Cayman River. Unknown to the villagers, the meteor is about to change their lives forever.

Chapter 1

A Meteorite Lands in the River

Water is life. To say that one drop of water is insignificant,
Is to say that one's life is insignificant.

Unknown

The Meteor silently landed in the Cayman River. The villagers noticed when the Meteor streaked across the sky, but they didn't hear it when it landed, so they continued on with their evening activities.

There was no noticeable physical change or physical activities in the river. As time passed, the fall season approached, and the fish in the river began to multiply in large numbers, and the Indian villagers thought they were blessed. The increase in fish meant they would have plenty of food to carry them through the harsh upcoming winter.

As the winter season approached, it was very cold with frequent blizzards. Even with their bountiful catch of fish earlier, there was very little food, so the villagers went to the Indian chief Running Bear, so he sent out a hunting party and they were gone for two days hunting for meat. They returned without any meat so the Indian chief told everyone not to worry, that the river was still full of fish, and he assured them they would not starve that the river was blessed by the gods and it would feed all of their people.

The villagers continued to eat the fish from the river and they noticed the fish were an unusual blue color. Everyone ate the fish and they noticed that the fish tasted better than the regular fish that they usually ate from the river. The blue fish tasted sweet.

The men in the village noticed that they wanted to mate more often. Most of the women in the village became pregnant. Even the chief's wife became pregnant. Her name was Sunny.

Most of the women in the village started feeling sick, and the medicine man noticed that most of the woman's stomachs were larger than normal and he offered them some medicine but they all refused to take it.

Chief Running Bear convinced his wife Sunny to take the medication. She trusted her husband and took it.

The fish didn't affect any of the kids in the village; it only affected adults. After a few days, all the women's pregnancy pains went away.

The medicine man went to the chief and told him that something was wrong and that all the women's stomachs were bigger than what they should be; he said most of the women were two or three months pregnant, but they looked like they were four or five months pregnant.

The villagers didn't suspect the blue fish was the problem, so they continued to eat the fish from the Cayman River.

Sunny was the only villager that stopped eating the fish from the river. She would go out and hunt for her own meat, which was mostly rabbits, chickens, and ducks. She also ate nuts and fruits.

The villagers wondered why there were no wild animals around that they could capture for meat. The hunting party would go out every day but return empty handed.

All the villagers still lived a normal and happy life. The village chief forbade Sunny from taking long walks in the forest in search for food.

Sunny defied his orders and continued hunting in the woods. Sunny constantly talked to her stomach, and sang to her baby. She knew her baby would be special. She braided a special ankle bracelet for it, a duplicate bracelet that she wore on her ankle.

After a few months passed, Sunny began to sleep-walk and wander through the forest every night, so Chief Running Bear had to keep a close eye on her.

After a few months of a bad winter, spring was about to arrive, and the fish started to return to their normal color. The villagers continued to eat the fish from the Cayman River.

Most of the village women knew something was wrong, because it was taking too long for them to go into labor to have their babies. They went to see the village medicine man and he could not explain why they were still pregnant. He told them that, when the babies were ready, they would come out on their own.

The Indian chief told everyone to continue their daily activities as spring arrived and no babies were born.

Sunny continued to hunt for meat, still refusing to eat the fish from the river. Her husband, Chief Running Bear tried to convince her that the fish in the river was ok to eat. She told him, "then you eat it," and she still refused to eat the fish. She could feel her baby move inside of her, when the other women could not feel their babies move.

Sunny continued to sing to her baby and take long walks in the woods. The late-night sleep-walking stopped, and she was happy. The sleep-walking had begun to get dangerous because no one knew she was doing it.

Sunny became worried because she felt better, with a lot of extra energy. She was resting late one night, and she started seeing visions but decided not to tell her husband because she thought the visions would pass.

She didn't tell anyone about the visions, because she thought they would think she was crazy.

Summer arrived and it was early in the morning and Sunny started feeling a sharp pain in her stomach and, as she stood up, blood started running down her leg and she turned to her husband Running Bear and said it was time.

Chief Running Bear ran out of the tent to get the medicine man. Everyone else was also running out of their tents trying to get the medicine man.

The medicine man just stood in the middle of the small village and thought to himself, *This is unbelievable; every pregnant woman in the village decides to go into labor at the same time.*

Chief Running Bear said, "I am the Chief and you will take care of my wife first."

The medicine man said, "No, we will put everyone in the largest tent, and I will treat all of them at the same time." So all of the pregnant women were taken to the tent and the chief went back to his tent to get his wife. They went to the large tent and the women were all screaming in pain.

Sunny didn't scream; she just breathed heavily. One by one, all of the Indian women delivered dead blue babies. All the women cried, and the medicine man asked all of them if they wanted to hold their dead babies, but they all refused.

Sunny was the last one in labor to deliver her baby, a boy, and the medicine man asked her if she wanted to hold her dead baby. Although the chief said "no," Sunny said, "Yes, please give me my baby, and she held him and sang to him the same song that she always sang to him as tears rolled down her face and dripped onto her baby face. Unknown to Sunny, her baby was not dead, but he was only in a deep sleep because he was special.

Chief Running Bear asked the medicine man to take all the babies and put them in the Cayman River.

The medicine man asked why the river. "Shouldn't we just bury them or burn them and spread the ashes in the river?"

"No," the chief said, "The river is the cause of this problem, because our people ate the blue fish; the problem came from the river, so it is only right that we should send the problem back to the river."

The medicine man said, "Ok, I will start collecting all the dead babies and start preparing them."

Sunny took the ankle bracelet that she had made for her baby and put it around his ankle and she gave him one last kiss as the tears streamed down her face.

Chief Running Bear had to pull the baby from her arms and place the baby with the others. All the Indian women had brought woven baskets with them for their delivered babies, but instead, the baskets had became their caskets.

The medicine man and Chief Running Bear and several other men placed all the babies in their baskets and placed them in the river as the priestess gave all the babies their last rites. As the babies were placed in the river, all the village people stood on the river bank, saddened because of the twenty babies' deaths.

Fifty miles down-river lived the brother of Chief Running Bear who had been exiled from the village. His name was Jim Bo and his wife's name was Cheyenne Bo. Jim Bo had been exiled because he was a warrior and wanted to be chief. Jim Bo was exiled to the edge of the mountain near the Cayman River.

He saw the smoke signals that indicated there was a death in the village.

Jim Bo was outside on that sunny day with his beautiful, youthful wife, strolling down the river bank. Cheyenne noticed all the baby baskets floating down river toward them. As the babies floated by, Sunny's baby woke up from his deep sleep because of the sound of the wolves howling. The wolves were running along the river bank to head off the floating baby baskets.

Sunny's baby started to cry, and Cheyenne heard it, and she asked her husband, "Did you hear a baby cry?" but he said no. Then she heard the cry again, so she ran into the icy cold river and told her husband that one of the babies was crying and was still alive. They stopped each and every baby basket to find out which baby was alive and crying.

Cheyenne was sick to her stomach and crying because she had to look at the faces of all the dead babies. As they stood in the river and checked each basket, they realized each one was dead, and so they let the baskets continue on down the river, to let the river consume them. Cheyenne thrashed frantically about through the water, trying to find out which baby was alive.

Sunny's baby was the last one floating down the river but, at that time, he had stopped crying, enjoying the sound of the river water.

As Cheyenne grabbed the last basket, the baby just looked up at her and smiled. Cheyenne just held the basket gazing at the beautiful light-blue skinned baby boy.

Jim Bo asked her to let go of the basket. He said it was no use, all the babies were dead, but Cheyenne said, "No, this one is alive and he is a beautiful baby boy."

Cheyenne told her husband the baby had been sent from heaven because she could not have any children.

Jim Bo told his wife that they must return the baby to the village, but again, she said, "No, they didn't want him because they put him in the river so the river would consume him."

She told her husband, "You can't ever go back to the village, because you have been exiled. We must keep him and raise him as our own, and I don't care if he is blue," and as they looked toward the river bank, it was lined with what looked like over a hundred wolves. "They want the baby," Jim Bo said.

Cheyenne clutched the basked closer. "I want to keep the baby, and I will not give him to them."

"They don't look like they're trying to attack us," Jim Bo said. "Maybe if we walk slowly they will let us pass. They walked up to the wolves, and the wolf pack moved away to let them pass.

The alpha male howled, and all the wolves backed away and started running away; then the alpha male wolf stopped and stared at Jim Bo and Cheyenne and then ran away.

Jim Bo and his wife took the baby home but did not realize that the wolves were secretly not far behind them.

The wolves followed them in the tree line. Jim Bo and Cheyenne went home with the baby, and Cheyenne held the baby very close to her bosom. They both noticed that the baby never cried while she was holding him. When they arrived home with the baby, she tried to feed the baby some goat's milk, but he refused to drink it; she tried to feed him some cow's milk, but he refused to drink that, too. She began to worry, because the baby refused to eat or drink milk, although he still would not cry.

Jim Bo and Cheyenne were up all night, worrying about the baby's health. The next morning, they left the baby in the tent and went out to get some food. Jim went hunting for meat, while Cheyenne milked the goat again.

While they were both busy, a nursing female she-wolf crept into the tent and laid down beside the baby and tugged on the baby garment and tried to get him to feed. The baby was in a position where he couldn't feed, so the nursing female wolf stood over the baby with her breast dangling over the baby, but the baby still couldn't reach the wolf's breast. The female wolf decided to squat down over the baby, and the baby started feeding and sucking the wolf's breast.

Jim Bo and Cheyenne returned to the tent and were startled to see the wolf standing over the baby while the baby was feeding from her. They tried to get the wolf to move away from the baby, but the wolf growled and started displaying her fangs as if she was trying to protect the baby.

Jim Bo looked into the wolf's eyes and saw the sensitivity there.

He told Cheyenne, "The wolf won't hurt the baby, so please let the baby finish feeding." After the baby finished feeding, the wolf just walked out of the tent and back into the woods, where there were other wolves waiting.

Cheyenne asked Jim Bo why the baby would only feed from a female wolf and not a goat or cow.

"I don't know," Jim Bo replied, "but I will bring the goat in and we'll see if the baby will drink from the goat's breast, and Cheyenne told him to wait until later, because the baby had just been fed.

Jim Bo told Cheyenne the wolves would return.

Cheyenne said, "I don't think the wolves mean us harm and, somehow, they are connected to the baby."

Jim Bo told Cheyenne, "We need to name the baby."

Cheyenne said, "We will call him Bo," and Jim Bo said, "That is a good name for him." Later in the evening, they brought the goat into the tent to feed the baby, but the baby Bo refused to suck the breast of the goat. They brought the cow into the tent and he still refused to feed.

Cheyenne refused to sleep and held the baby all through the night. Cheyenne fell in love with the baby Bo, and she wished that she had given birth to him.

The next morning, the she wolf returned, waiting outside the tent, so Jim Bo and Cheyenne brought Bo outside and laid him on the ground with a blanket, and the she wolf walked up and stood over baby Bo and squatted so he could feed, and he began suckling right away. Cheyenne just smiled and held her husband and said the baby would be fine. "The wolf is acting like a mother to him."

So Jim Bo told Cheyenne, "We'll continue to do this every day, if this is what it will take for baby Bo to survive. Day after day, the wolf would return to feed baby Bo.

After three months, the she wolf could no longer feed baby Bo because she was not producing any more milk, but another nursing wolf took her place, while the other wolves either stood guard or lay near the tree line. The wolf pack numbered around a hundred or so clan members and, for some reason, they protected baby Bo.

"This is very unusual," Jim Bo told Cheyenne, "for this many wolves to travel in packs this large. They can't be from the same pack. There is something very unusual about baby Bo for all these wolves to have so much interest in protecting him. The she-wolves are taking turns feeding him, because he is beginning to drink more milk than they can produce. "We are going to have to wean him from drinking so much milk. He's almost six months old, and he is very strong and beginning to learn how to walk; so we must start feeding him meat."

* * *

After baby Bo started eating meat, the she wolves stopped breast feeding him and, as he grew stronger, he started walking at seven months old. The wolves continued to visit the Bo family tent area. Baby Bo, Jim Bo, and Cheyenne got used to the wolves visiting baby Bo. Baby Bo was now a year old and he was walking and talking. He was growing very fast, even faster than a normal child. Jim Bo and Cheyenne noticed it, but they kept quiet because they loved baby Bo greatly.

Cheyenne saw that the wolves were so protective of baby Bo that she let him play with the wolves and wander off with them, but she would not let him travel too far. She would only let him travel with the wolves as far as she could see, then she would call out to him not to travel any farther. Baby Bo spent most of his time playing with the wolves' cubs.

Chapter 2

Adjustments

Everyone's life is filled with secrets

Jim Bo

As time went on, baby Bo required less feeding from the female wolves and he started eating regular food. He ate meat, fruit, nuts, and other foods. Baby Bo's skin began to turn to its original color as his dominant DNA genes began to take over. Baby Bo always followed the wolves around everywhere they went, but his mother refused to let him out of her sight. As baby Bo learn to walk and began to talk, his mother constantly stayed close to him.

She would always talk to him and sing him to sleep at night. The wolves still visited the camp site every day.

By the time Bo was seven years old, his father Jim Bo started taking him out hunting and fishing. He taught Bo all the ways of hunting. Bo was a fast learner. He loved his mother Cheyenne, but Bo constantly had dreams about his real birth mother; but he didn't know what the dreams meant, because they were all jumbled up in his mind.

Bo was also beginning to have problems controlling his thoughts, because he could hear all the thoughts of all the animals in the forest.

His mother noticed he was having nightmares, as he constantly tossed and turned in his bed at night as he slept.

Cheyenne told Jim Bo she couldn't take it anymore and she couldn't continue to watch Bo suffer. She said, "We need to help him with his dreams and teach him how to control his thoughts."

Jim Bo told Cheyenne to give Bo a little more time. He explained how boys liked to solve their own problems.

Cheyenne said, "No, we are his parents, and it's our duty to look after him and take good care of him."

Jim Bo disagreed. "Let's give him a chance to come to us for help."

She told Jim Bo, "Ok, I will give him a little more time, but if he doesn't come to me for help, then I will go to him, because he is my son and I love him so much. I don't want to let anything happen to him. As time passed, Bo simply became withdrawn because there were no other children around to play with and grow up with. Bo began to spend more time with the wolves. He used most of his time running with them. He began to understand the sounds in his head, and he could understand what the other animals were saying to him. As time went on, he grew even stronger.

Cheyenne was cooking dinner, and Bo walked up behind her and gave her a big hug, surprising Cheyenne. She told Bo that he was getting very big, and anytime he needed to talk and spend time with her, she would always be available.

The female wolf was like a third mother to Bo. The wolf had one more cub, and she arrived at the Bo family tent early one morning with the cub in her mouth.

Bo was sitting outside with his mother and father. Bo looked up and sensed something was wrong; there were no other wolves around, and the she-wolf stood there all alone with her cub, which she laid on the ground.

Bo ran to her right away as she gently laid the cub in his hands. Bo could hear her thoughts as she told him she was dying, and she wanted him to raise her cub, because she couldn't. The she-wolf lay on the ground, closed her eyes, and took her last breath and died. Bo started crying; tears rolled down his face asking her not to leave him.

Cheyenne told Bo the she-wolf had died knowing her cub would be well taken care of.

Jim Bo asked Bo why she died, and he said she died of old age and she wanted me to raise her cub because the wolf pack would kill him without her.

"I will keep the promise that I just made to her," Bo said. "I will raise the cub as my brother."

The wolf pack arrived, wanting the cub, but Bo said no and pointed in the opposite direction, asking the pack to leave. The lead wolf growled and showed his fangs and attacked Bo. Bo threw the cub to Jim Bo and wrestled the dominant male wolf to the ground and held him down, and all the other wolves started growling and showing their fangs, getting ready to attack.

Bo looked up and growled back, with two-inch fangs hanging from his mouth, and his eyes turned from brown to grey. All the wolves backed away with fear. As Bo held the dominant male wolf down, he said, "My brother, I will never ever hurt you or anyone in the pack, but you must never challenge me again, for I am Bo, dominant male leader of the wolf pack." The alpha male wolf just lay still and submitted to Bo. Bo retracted his fangs and his eye's returned to their normal brown color. He patted the alpha male wolf and said, "Now all of you go home." The alpha male wolf trotted away, but he turned and growled. Bo looked him in his eyes and used his telepathic abilities to communicate with the wolf, and the wolf stopped growling, walked over to Bo, and licked his face and wagged his tail. Bo rubbed the wolf and told him, telepathically, *it's ok, now go home. I will visit all of you soon, but for now you are in charge.*

The alpha male wolf led the wolf pack away from the Bo family camp.

"Bo, what was that all about?" Cheyenne asked.

"I will explain later," Bo said, "but right now I must bury my mother."

"I am your mother," Cheyenne replied.

"I sense I have three mothers," Bo replied. "You, the she wolf, and someone else that I see in my dreams all the time. We'll talk later, because I need you to explain to me who this third person is. This is the only way to stop the dreams that enter my head every night; I see her crying and reaching her hands out to me. These dreams have a meaning, and I need to stop them once and for all. I have to go and bury the wolf; I will return in a little while and we can have the talk that you always said you wanted."

Bo asked his father to care for the cub until he returned.

"Don't worry," Jim Bo said. "I will look after the cub, so you just go and bury the wolf."

Bo took the wolf and carried her into the forest.

"What are we going to do?" Cheyenne said to Jim Bo.

"There is nothing we can do now," Jim Bo replied, "but explain to him the whole story about how we found him."

"But he will leave us on a quest, looking for his real mother," Cheyenne said and she started to cry.

"We have to tell him the truth," Jim Bo said. "He will understand. He is old enough to understand and he loves us both, so if he leaves, he will return, because this is the only home he knows. He will seek out his true mother and we can't try to stop him. We will tell him the whole story and point him in the right direction; he will follow his instincts and his vision. I know my son, and I know he loves you just as much as I love you. He will leave one day and he might find his real mother and father, but we are the only true mother and father he knows, so he will come back, I promise."

Cheyenne continued to cry in Bo's absence, while he was away burying the she wolf.

Jim Bo gave Cheyenne the wolf cub so it could comfort her. He told Cheyenne, "The she-wolf helped you raise your son, so maybe now you can return the favor."

She looked up and smiled and hugged Jim Bo very tight and said, "That's why I married you, because you always know how to make me feel happy."

Bo took the she-wolf to their favorite spot near the river; he cried as he buried her and said, "I will always love you."

Bo said, "I am now in my teen years and, in a few more years, I will run with the wolf pack." He finished burying the she-wolf and covered her with dirt and placed a large rock over her grave as a head stone, wiping away his tears, as he walked away looking back one last time.

Bo went back home through the forest and, as he walked, he thought to himself, *I will start training hard to be the best warrior a man can become. I will ask my father to train me.* Bo continued walking through the forest, but he could hear something following him. He heard footsteps in the distance, but they would never get too close. Bo knew the sound wasn't the wolf pack, so he continued walking home. He finally arrived home. His father was outside chopping wood, and he asked Bo if everything was all right.

"Something was following me in the forest, but it didn't get too close," Bo said.

"It was probably another wild animal, because you've always attracted wild animals and brought them home, ever since you were a small boy," Jim Bo said. "In time, the pain will pass," his father told him. "I know you loved her, but we all will die someday, including your mother and me. We saw something in you today that have your mother worried, but we will talk about it later."

Cheyenne came outside crying and Bo ran to her and hugged her. "I don't care what you are," Cheyenne said. "You are still my son." She looked Bo in his brown eyes then she took her fingers and parted his lips to check for his fangs. "Please tell me you are still my Bo."

"I will always be your Bo, mother." Bo looked up at her sad eyes and said, "We all must talk, you, me, and father."

Cheyenne said, "Here, take your little friend and sit down." Cheyenne tried to explain how she found him, but Bo stopped her.

"Let me explain some of the things about me first," Bo said.

But Jim Bo said, "No, let me and your mother talk first, and you will better understand why you are who you are. Your mother and I are from a small village north of here at the base of the mountains. I was exiled from the village many years ago because my brother and I both wanted to be chief of the village. We fought and I won, and I badly injured him.

"The people in the village however chose him to be chief, so he exiled me from the village, but it was not out of hatred. He exiled me because he loved me, and he knew we both could not be chief, so it was best that I leave.

"Your mother loves me so much that she decided to leave with me, knowing I could never return. Your mother's sister married my brother. I am a warrior, and if I had stayed in the village, it would have divided the village, so it was best that I left."

Then Cheyenne told Bo that something bad had happened at the village. "Your father and I were walking along the river bank one day, and we saw all these baby baskets floating down the river.

"All the babies' skin was blue, and they were all dead, but we heard one of the babies crying, but we couldn't figure out which one was alive, so we had to check every baby basket because they were all heading toward the water falls."

"Why were all the babies' skin blue?" Bo asked

Jim Bo and Cheyenne said we don't know. "We searched all the baskets, and you were the last one, and the only one that was alive, so we plucked you out of the river and took you home with us, blue skin and all. We thought you were going to die, because you would not eat for weeks and you wouldn't cry. We tried feeding you cow's milk, goat's milk, and meat, but you wouldn't eat."

"Honey," Jim Bo said, "you forgot the part about the wolves at the river bank."

"Yes," Cheyenne said, "when we plucked you from the river, there were hundreds of wolves standing at the river bank, but they never attacked and, as we exited the river, they parted and followed us home, but they always stayed in the tree line and forest. It was as if they were trying to protect you. And when you would not eat, it was the she-wolf that sneaked into the tent and breastfed you. We knew if we wanted to keep you alive, we would have to continue to let her breast feed you, because you refused to eat anything else, and she returned every day to continue to feed you until you were strong and, when she could not feed you anymore, she brought another nursing she-wolf to continue feeding you until you stopped drinking breast milk. That is probably how you came to be who you are."

"It's ok, mother, you can say it; I am part wolf. You were right, father. Now I can better understand everything that is going on in my head. The visions of the woman I keep seeing in my dreams is probably down in the village. And I will go to the village someday, mother, but not right now, because I see that it bothers you too much. I will go in a few years when I'm older."

Cheyenne smiled and said, "Then you are my son. Even in a few years, you will still be my little Bo."

"I know, mother, another question, where did this band on my leg come from?"

"We don't know, but when we found you, it was on your leg. That band will probably connect you to your true mother. All the women in our village put those bands around their newborn babies' legs."

"What happened to my blue skin?"

"We don't know that, either. It just went away as you got older, before you turned a year old."

"Ok, last question, father, will you teach me how to become a warrior like you?"

"Yes, I will teach you everything I know," Jim Bo replied.

Cheyenne told Bo, "Now that you know everything, what will you do?"

"I will keep my word. I will train with father and raise the wolf cub, and then, in a few years, I will go seek my real mother, and then I will return home."

Chapter 3

Warrior Training

No man can be asked to do more
Than his best even if he falls short.

Bo was now seventeen years old and began his warrior training every day. His father would take him into the forest and train him in the art of hunting and animal tracking.

Bo didn't spend any time with the wolf pack, but they still ran free in the forest hunting in packs. The wolves stayed away from the Bo family camp.

Bo continued the training with his father; his father taught him how to throw knives, throw a boomerang, shoot a crossbow, and combat knife fighting. Bo trained with his father for a year.

His father told him, "I have taught you all that I know, so now the rest of the training is up to you."

Bo used a lot of his time doing things with his wolf friend, who was now full grown, and they went everywhere together. The following spring, Bo had a sad look on his face, and Cheyenne asked him what was wrong. Bo told her that the time was getting near for him to leave home for a little while to continue his training.

Cheyenne told Bo, "I knew this day was coming and that you would want to seek out your birth mother."

"No, mother," Bo said. "I will be going farther south, higher into the mountains. I want to continue my training uninterrupted. I'll leave my wolf here at home with you and dad, until I return."

"No," Cheyenne said, "if you are going to leave, you will need a friend and a companion to keep you company and to look after you. When will you be leaving?"

"In a few days," Bo said.

Jim Bo asked Bo, "Did you ever give your wolf a name, because I never hear you call him?"

"I don't have to call him," Bo said, "because he follows me everywhere I go. But, Dad, his name is Fang."

"Come here, Fang," Jim Bo said, and the wolf walked over to him.

Cheyenne called Fang and he went over to her.

"You see? Fang is a part of this family and loves both of you," Bo said.

"I know what you are trying to do," Cheyenne said, "But I want you to take Fang with you on your journey."

Later that night, Bo was asleep and he saw a vision of his true mother, again, and he woke up, realizing the visions were getting stronger and stronger, as he wiped the sweat off of his face. Bo knew that, one day, he would have to take a trip to find his birth mother.

The next day, Bo decided to go for a walk in the forest, and when he was a little way into the forest, he heard footsteps again, but this time, as he turned around, he saw it was a horse as white as snow following him. He thought to himself, *this is really strange*, so he went up to the horse, and the horse was not afraid of him and Bo patted him and rubbed him and said, "Sorry, friend, but I don't need a ride." But, as Bo turned to walk away, the horse followed him. Bo thought, *well, I guess father was right once again. All the animals are attracted to me.* As he walked away, the horse continued to follow him all the way home.

When Bo arrived home, Jim Bo looked up at his wife. "Your son has brought home another mouth to feed," he said, and Cheyenne started laughing when she saw the horse, because she knew all animals were attracted to Bo.

Once Bo reached the tent, his father said, "I will teach you how to ride him tomorrow."

It was very easy for Bo to learn how to ride the horse, because the horse followed Bo's every command. The following week, Bo gathered some clothing and food and kissed his mother goodbye, and he took his wolf and horse and rode farther up into the mountains on his journey. Bo waved goodbye to his parents as he disappeared into the forest.

Cheyenne cried and Jim Bo assured her that Bo would be just fine. "Your little boy is growing up fast," he said.

Bo had been gone for months, and Cheyenne was still crying as she waited for Bo to come walking out of the forest, but he never showed up.

Winter was now setting in, and Bo was still up in the mountains. He continued to hunt and live off the land. Every day, Bo practiced his warrior combat moves, and he exercised and lifted heavy rocks to increase his muscle size. One day, Bo and Fang decided to hunt a deer and, as the deer began to run, Bo and the wolf chased it; after awhile, Bo realized they had been chasing the deer for hours, and he wasn't even tired. Bo finally exhausted the deer and cornered it and, when he looked into the deer's eyes, Bo could feel so much fear and pain that he dropped to his knees and raised his hands to the sky and said, "I now understand the gift. I was put here to be part of the wilderness. I am part of the forest; we are as one. I am part man and part animal, so it will be my job to protect the animals; no, I am still part man, so I will live with the animals, but I will not interfere with the animal's way of life."

Bo turned and walked away from the deer. "Come. Let's go, Fang. Let's run some more," and they continued running through the mountain and forest.

During, the next few months, they lived off fish, fruits, and nuts. Bo found a cave, and he told Fang it would be their new home until winter was over.

Bo continued to exercise, and his keen eyesight increased, along with his sense of smell. Bo continued to travel around the mountains, hunting and living off the land, but he never saw any people. He still practiced throwing his boomerang and he practiced knife throwing. He perfected every skill that his father Jim Bo had taught him. Bo and Fang continued running through the forest. Bo could run for miles without stopping for food or water.

It was now springtime, and a few years had now passed, and Bo was now twenty-one years old and the size of a full grown man, compared to the scrawny teenage boy he had been years ago. Bo and Fang were walking through the forest, and Bo could smell human blood and he could smell wolves. Then he heard two girls screaming, so he and Fang raced off in the direction of the screams.

It was a small wolf pack circling the two girls. Bo told Fang to protect the girls as one of the wolves tried to attack them. Fang and the attacking wolf started fighting as Bo used his boomerang to make a weird noise as it banked off the ground and trees and back into his hand. The wolves started circling Bo and the two girls, while Fang was still fighting with the other wolf. Bo grabbed the attacking wolf, careful not to hurt him, and he slung the wolf into the bushes. The wolves regrouped to attack again, but Bo went into a combat stance and his eyes turned grey and his fangs came out. He said, "That is enough. I want all of you to leave now," and as Bo looked from left to right, all the wolves retreated back into the tree line. Bo asked the two girls if they were hurt and they said no. "You did good, Fang, protecting the girls," Bo said. "Thank you, my friend."

The girls asked who he was and what he was as they cowered at the base of a large tree.

"It doesn't matter who I am or what I am," Bo said, as he retracted his fangs and his eyes turned back to brown. "I just want to make sure you are safe. If the wolves hurt you, then other people will hunt and hurt the wolves, and we don't need these kinds of problems. The wolves were hungry, but they will hunt somewhere else. Both of you will be safe, so please go home and please don't tell anyone about what you saw. You can tell them about the wolves, but don't tell them about me."

The girls promised not to tell anyone about Bo's transformation.

Then Bo and Fang ran in the opposite direction.

One of the girls turned and said, "What is your name?" and he turned around and said, "Bo. Now please go home."

As Bo returned to the cave, he thought to himself, *this is another lesson learned; now I have to be careful how I reveal myself. I will have to learn to keep the wolf part of me hidden.* Bo and Fang went to the river, because Bo could sense and smell the wolf pack was near. "I must feed my brothers and sisters," Bo said, so he went to the river and started catching fish. As the wolf pack came closer, Bo threw fish to them, and they all started eating. Bo caught plenty of fish to make sure that all the wolves were well fed. After that, Bo and Fang left and went back to the cave.

Bo continued running the next day, and then he rode his horse for a few days. Bo was still having bad dreams and visions of the real mother that he needed to visit. It was now close to summer, and Bo and Fang were resting near the cave, but Fang kept whining, so Bo looked into Fang's eyes and said, "You know I can read your mind, and I know what you are thinking.

"Fang, I would also like to see Cheyenne and Jim Bo, because I miss them, too. I have to complete my training. But I guess we can go back a little early, and we can also visit our brothers and sisters in the wolf pack and spend a little time with them. I owe them my life. We have been gone a long time, but I'm sure they will still remember us. We'll leave in the morning to go home."

With that, Bo packed up his gear for the long trip home the next morning. When Bo went to sleep, he dreamed and saw images of his real, natural mother, and he saw how beautiful she was. Bo also saw how sad she was and, every time he saw a vision of her, she was crying. Bo didn't know that what he was seeing was actually happening at that moment and that it was not a dream. He was telepathically connected to his birth mother. Bo's mother had been crying over his death since the day he was born; she had been crying for twenty-one years over the death of her son, although she did not know that, in reality, he was not dead.

Bo woke up from the dream, sweating. The dreams and visions were getting stronger and happening more frequently.

Bo sat up and closed his eyes, as if he was trying to control the vision in his mind. After a short while, the vision was under control, and so, early that morning, he packed all of his stuff on his horse and headed down the mountain. After traveling a half a day, Bo and Fang finally arrived at the wolves' den. The wolves were out hunting. A few she-wolves were at the den watching the cubs and, when Bo and Fang approached, the wolves jumped to their feet. One of the she-wolves recognized Bo and ran to him, very happy to see him. Bo sat down on the ground as all the she wolves gathered around and greeted him to welcome him back into the pack.

The wolves also welcomed Fang, as well. Bo played with all the pups, while most of the she-wolves lay near Bo. And then, the male wolves returned from hunting. They noticed Bo and Fang and they started growling, and Fang started growling back, but Bo told everyone to stop. "We are all brothers and sisters and we will not fight. The alpha male wolf walked over to Bo and sniffed him, even though he recognized Bo; he wanted to be sure Bo was who he appeared to be. The alpha male wolf sniffed Bo again, and Bo grabbed him and hugged him, and said, "I know you remember me. I'm sorry it's been a long time, but I have been far away, but now I'm back, and I will not leave you again. I will come to visit you more often. You also know where I live, so you can come and visit me sometimes."

Bo and Fang spent the night with the wolves, but at the break of dawn, he decided to leave and head home to visit Jim Bo and Cheyenne. Once he arrived home, he saw that they were both outside picking vegetables from the garden. Cheyenne was tugging on some vegetables and had to tug real hard, so when she raised her arm, Fang crept up behind her and poked his head under her armpit. Cheyenne was so surprised she called out to Jim Bo who came running and saw Fang in Cheyenne's arms.

Jim Bo looked up and saw Bo coming from the forest. Cheyenne ran to Bo, hugging and kissing him. "WOW!" she said, "You have grown so big. Please tell me you are going to stay home, because I missed you so much," and then she started to cry.

Bo tried to wipe away her tears and comfort Cheyenne while telling her stories about his journey.

Cheyenne asked Bo about his dreams, and he said his dreams were getting worse.

For the next few weeks, Bo stayed close to home with his mother. One day, the wolf pack arrived, and Bo stood up and stripped off all of his clothes right in front of his mother and father and, to their surprise, Bo and Fang just ran off into the forest and ran with the wolf pack.

"That boy is unbelievable," Jim Bo said. "You see how he just stripped off all of his clothes and ran off into the forest."

"He is strange, but I love him just the same and with all my heart," Cheyenne said.

Bo and Fang ran with the other wolves and they hunted in the forest, but Bo would not kill or eat other animals. Bo and Fang returned home late that night. Cheyenne was still up and about because she could not sleep, and she fed them both.

Bo slept quietly most of the night, but the dreams came again. The next morning, Bo told Cheyenne and Jim Bo that the dreams and visions were getting worse. He told his parents he had to go to his birth place, because this was the reason for the dreams. Bo figured if he returned to his birth place, maybe the dreams would stop.

Cheyenne agreed and said, "I understand, but only if it will help me get my son back. I want you to do whatever you think is right for you and whatever it takes to stop the bad dreams and visions."

Bo and Jim Bo went for a long walk the next day. Bo explained to his father that he must go to the family village to get some answers to the dreams and visions.

Jim Bo explained to Bo that his mother worried a lot for his safety.

"She doesn't have to worry," Bo said, "Because I can handle myself. You have taught me well."

"No, Bo, that's not it; she worries all the time about losing you as a son."

"Mother will never lose me. I will always be her son, and I will always love her."

"You just don't understand, Bo; you lost one mother and you cried for days, so just keep in mind how your mother will feel if she loses you, either in death or to another woman. You lost one mother, and you are somehow attached or mentally linked to another mother who abandoned you as a newborn baby. When you return to the village, you will probably find something you might not like."

Bo said, "I promise that no matter what happens, this is my home and this is where I will live with you, Cheyenne, and the wolves. You and Cheyenne are my true mother and father. I just need to go to the village to get some answers to stop these dreams and visions; otherwise, I will be no good to anyone if I go out of my mind."

"I understand," Jim Bo said. "Please just don't disappoint your mother because you will break her heart."

"I promise I will return home and I will never do anything to hurt my mother."

"I know," Jim Bo said, "But it's not me you need to convince, it is your mother."

"I don't know what else to do to prove to her that I love her."

"Just be her son," Jim Bo said. When they returned to the camp, Bo walked up to Cheyenne and looked her in her eyes and said, "I love you mother, with all my heart," and then he kissed her gently on the lips and gave her a comforting hug and just held her, as she began to cry, and he whispered in her ear, "Mother, I promise to return home," he said, continuing to hold her. Later that night, Bo slept outside under the stars with Fang and all the other wolves.

Jim Bo and Cheyenne were in the tent, lying in bed. Jim Bo held Cheyenne while she cried.

"Bo will be ok," Jim Bo told her. "He doesn't know what else to do but go to the village for some answers, and I think he is doing the right thing, and you know he is doing the right thing, and I love him with all my heart."

"I know he is my sister's son, but I don't want to lose him to her. She is manipulative and I know she is going to try to take him back."

"Bo is a grown young man now," Jim Bo explained, "And he has to make his own decisions, and I have faith in him, because we have taught him well. We can't push him; we can only guide him. And another thing, his wolves will not be accepted in that village and you and I both know Bo will not be separated from his wolves."

Jim Bo snuggled in close to Cheyenne and told her to please get some sleep, as he held her close.

Chapter 4

Bo Returns to His Place of Birth

*Hatred should not be so easy,
nor forgiveness so difficult.*

The following day, Bo mounted his horse and took Fang as they traveled toward the village. The wolf pack followed along the tree line in the forest, but Bo told them not to follow. Bo traveled through the forest with Fang and decided the trip would be faster if he traveled along the river bank. Bo and Fang traveled a half a day along the river bank. Bo could now see the Indian village off in the distance, so he decided to travel across the prairie. Once Bo and Fang reached the prairie, everything began to smell different, and Bo knew they were close to the Indian village. As Bo crossed the prairie, he could hear a woman's muffled screams. Bo still took his time. He was curious what was going on, so he continued moving toward the sound. Suddenly, Bo saw two white men wrestling with a woman, but Bo decided to turn around, because it was not any of his business what was going on.

But the woman screamed out, "Please help me!"

But Bo kept on riding in the opposite direction, and then the women screamed again, "Please help me!" then

Fang turned around and ran toward the two men, growling ferociously.

The two men released the woman, and Bo saw that she was an Indian, so he went back.

"Kill the wolf," one of the men said to the other.

Bo rode up on his white horse and said, "My friend Fang doesn't like it when you attack helpless women. Me, personally, I don't care what you do, but now we want you to release her."

The men said, "Boy if you want to keep on living, you better keep on riding that pretty white horse of yours."

Bo got down off of his horse. "I won't ask you again to release the woman." Now, Bo could smell the wolf pack, and he looked along the tree line and smiled. "If both of you want to continue living, you will release the woman," Bo said.

One of the men said, "We don't think you can beat both of us."

"I think I can," Bo said, "But I don't have to, because my brothers and sisters will take care of you." Both of the men looked over at the tree line at over fifty wolves inching toward Bo. Bo pointed toward the men and the wolves started circling them. The Indian woman was afraid of all of the wolves and she started cowering on the ground. The two men started running as the wolves gave chase.

Bo walked up to the woman and said, "It's ok, you are safe now."

As the Indian woman looked up, Bo stepped back. "It's you," he said. And the woman said, "Yes, I'm me, but who are you? And thank you for saving me."

"But it's you," Bo said again, and the woman again said, "Yes. I'm me, but who are you? You are an Indian but you are not from my village."

"My name is Bo."

"Well Bo, it's nice to meet you," the woman said, "and thank you again for saving me, but I must get home."

"You are so beautiful," Bo said.

"Thank you, again, but I must get home," the woman said. "You are very young to be so brave." She looked at Bo from head to toe, then she noticed the bracelet on Bo's ankle. "Where did you get that ankle bracelet?"

"It's mine," Bo replied. "I have worn it all my life."

The woman said, "I made only two of those bracelets. I have one on my ankle, and I placed the other one on my baby's ankle when he was born." She then pointed at her ankle to show Bo the ankle bracelet. The ankle bracelets matched.

"Where is your son?" Bo asked.

"He died at child birth. That's why I want to know how you got his ankle bracelet."

"My mother and father found me in the river many years ago. They told me there were about twenty dead babies floating down the river, and I was the only one alive. They saved me and raised me as their own."

The Indian woman finally noticed the physical resemblance that Bo reflected in herself and the chief. Was this really her son? She said, "No," as she dropped to her knees crying. "It can't be; you are my son that was supposed to have died many years ago. I thought you were dead, along with all the other babies. Your father and the medicine man had to pry you from my arms after they told me you were dead. Your father and the village medicine man put all the dead babies in the river, including you, because the fish in the river were the cause of all their deaths. They told me you were dead; you had blue skin, along with all the other babies. All the babies were born dead, but you were the only one that was born alive; then you stopped breathing in my arms and we thought you had also died. At least we thought you had died. I still cry to this day, longing to hold you in my arms, because I love you so much."

"I know," Bo said. "I see you and your pain in my in my visions every night, so much that I can't sleep. I have been having these visions of you for as long as I can remember; that is how I recognized you as soon as I saw your face. My father Jim Bo and mother Cheyenne pointed me to your village to look for answers. They would have traveled with me, but my father was exiled from your village."

"I know," the woman said. "I know all about it, because Cheyenne is my sister and Jim Bo is your father's brother. My name is Sunny."

Sunny cried and Bo told her it was a strange story. "But since that is the truth, then I have found what I was looking for; so now I can return home to my mother and father."

"No!" Sunny cried out. "I am your true mother and the chief of the village is your true father."

Bo asked Sunny if she knew about his condition, and Sunny said, "Yes, all the babies were blue. We ate blue fish from the river one year and we found out later that something was wrong with the fish, and so many women were pregnant that ate the fish and, when all the babies were born, they all were born dead."

"No," Bo said, "It's more than that."

"So what else is wrong with you?" Sunny asked. "Please don't tell me you are dying."

"No," Bo said, "I am half wolf and I can talk to the animals; that's why all the wolves were here. They were here to protect me. I was raised by them."

"I thought you said my sister raised you."

"She did, but she also said that I would not feed, and the only way I would feed was by a she-wolf's breast milk, until I was a year old, and we think that's how I got these weird senses. These senses are a part of me, so I am stuck with them."

"My village is your home and birth place," Sunny said.

"No, my home is in the mountains with my mother Cheyenne and father Jim Bo. I also love my brothers and sisters in the wolf pack who helped raise me," Bo said, "But I will make sure you get back to your village safely."

Sunny hugged Bo and cried.

Bo lifted her up and put her on his horse and climbed up on the horse with her and they rode slowly back to her village. As Sunny and Bo approached the village, everyone was watching them. All the village dogs started barking, but none of them would approach Fang.

Bo took one look at all the village dogs and they all stopped barking and scampered away.

Sunny sat proudly on top of the white horse, while Bo held her in his strong arms. Bo dismounted first, and then he helped Sunny down. Her dress was torn, and the chief walked up and asked Sunny what happened, but she slapped his face. "You lied to me; this young man saved me from two attackers."

The Indian chief pushed Sunny to the ground. "This is a lie; this is your lover that you have been sneaking off to see every day, and you thought I wouldn't find out," Chief Running Bear said, as he tried to strike her again while she was on the ground; but another Indian woman ran over to Sunny's defense; she was the medicine man's daughter and her name was Shana.

"This is not right," Shana said. Chief Running Bear tried to grab Sunny, but Bo stepped in between them and said, "That is enough."

The Chief stepped back and said, "I guess you want to take her punishment."

"I don't think you can win against me," Bo said.

Chief Running Bear rushed Bo, and they started fighting with knives. Bo wrestled the Chief to the ground, then all the other young Indian warriors approached with their knives and spears out, but the Indian Chief told the warriors to stay back.

Sunny crawled to both of the men. "Bo, please don't do this, because you will regret this in the future."

Bo looked at Sunny, saw that she was serious, and released the Indian chief, but he was still so upset that he took out his boomerang and flung it with great skill and cut off all the spearheads of the spears the young Indian warriors were holding. They were all surprised to see such skills.

The chief stood up and grabbed his staff and said, "I am not finished with you yet."

"I will not fight you," Bo replied, dropping all of his weapons and holding out his hands, then dropped to his knees.

The Indian chief went to strike Bo in the head with his staff, but Fang charged the chief, and Bo said, "No, Fang, stay."

Fang started howling and Bo said, "Stop, Fang, please quiet down."

The chief started to strike Bo, again, and the young Indian squaw Shana covered her body over Bo, and the chief struck Shana instead of Bo. He stopped. "Why is everyone trying to protect this young Bo? He is no leader."

Sunny said, "Please, husband, stop and take a close look at this young Bo."

"Why do I need to look at this young man who comes to my village and starts trouble, he who is also sleeping with my wife?" The chief said.

"That is not possible," Sunny said, "Because he is your son."

This boy is not my son," the chief said. "My son died many years ago."

"No, this is our son," Sunny insisted. "He was taken from the river that day, when you told me he was dead. Your brother Jim Bo and my sister Cheyenne raised him up in the mountain."

The Medicine man arrived and walked up and looked at Bo and examined his features, and then he looked at the chief. "It is possible that Bo could be your son."

Bo said, "No, my mother and father are Jim Bo and Cheyenne."

"Ok," the chief replied, "We will discuss this later. I might change my mind and kill him later."

"No you won't," Bo said, "Because my brothers and sisters will protect me."

"What brothers and sisters? I didn't even hit him in the head and he is talking crazy."

Bo waved his hand, and all the wolves came out of hiding, summoned when Fang howled. Bo waved his hand, again, and pointed; and the wolves took cover, again, in the bushes. Bo said, "They will stay hidden until I leave."

The chief said, "Good, then you can't stay here; you will have to stay in the woods with your brothers and sisters."

"No," Shana said. "Bo is a guest. My father and I have plenty of room in our tent, so he can stay with us."

Shana's father nodded. "Yes, I would like to hear Bo's story, so we can figure this mess out. Young Bo, come and bring the wolf with you."

Bo picked up all of his weapons and followed Shana and her father to their tent.

The chief said, "Come Sunny," but she refused.

"I will be staying with my son."

Sunny hugged Bo as they all walked back to Shana and her father's tent. All the other Indians were looking around to see where all the other wolves were hiding.

"Don't worry," Bo said, "They will not attack anyone; but they are there, you just can't see them."

Shana was walking with Bo, Sunny, and her father. "Where are you from?" Shana asked Bo, and he told her he was from up in the mountains, and she said, "Where in the mountains?"

"Nowhere in particular," he said. They continued their walk to Shana's tent.

Sunny asked Bo to tell her about how he grew up, and Shana also wanted to know more about Bo.

Shana whispered to Sunny, "You have a very handsome son, and he is also very nice."

Sunny said, "I wouldn't know, because this is the first time I have seen him since he was born." Once they arrived at the medicine man's tent, he started telling Bo the story of how all the babies from the village were born dead.

Shana decided to cook some food, and Sunny helped her. The medicine man told Bo that all the babies born dead that spring all had blue skin, because all the fish in the river were blue, and everyone ate the fish. "Something was wrong with the fish in the river that year. The next year everything cleared up, and that's when Shana was born. When Shana was born, her mother died giving birth to her. I tried all I could to save my wife.

"Shana is so beautiful, and she looks just like her mother. All the boys in the village keep asking me for her hand in marriage, but I leave that up to Shana, because she knows what kind of man she wants to marry."

When he finished telling his story, he looked at Bo. "Where did you get your wolf?" he asked. "Was he abandoned by his mother?"

"No," Bo said, "Fang's mother died, so she asked me to take care of him. Yes I can understand what all the animals say when they talk to me."

The medicine man thought Bo had hit his head when he was fighting with the chief.

Bo told the medicine man that Fang and all the other wolves were his brothers and sisters. He explained that, since the wolves saved his life as a baby, he was dedicated to them for the rest of his life. Bo told the medicine man that there were other strange things about him that he didn't understand.

The medicine man said, "Well, I am the village healer, so maybe I can help you with whatever sickness you have."

"I can hear what animals are thinking. I can see very far, and I can smell things that normal people can't."

Everyone sat down to eat, when Shana and Sunny passed out the food. Shana offered food to Fang, who ate from her hand.

"Shana," Bo said, "Fang just told me he likes you, and he said some other things, but I won't tell you what."

"You can really read animals' minds and talk to them?" Shana asked.

"Yes, Bo said.

Sunny asked Bo, "What else you can do?

"I can smell things, for example, that Shana is bleeding, but she is not cut," and everyone knew what he was talking about.

Shana was embarrassed, and Bo said, "I'm sorry. I didn't mean to embarrass you. I was only answering Sunny's question."

"Are you connected to the wolves?" Sunny asked.

Bo replied, "Yes," and explained how he was breast fed by the wolves when he was a baby. "Somehow, now, I can see and hear everything they do."

"Well, what else you can do?" Shana asked.

Bo said, "If I show you, it might frighten you."

But the medicine man said, "Well, show us anyway, because Shana is training to be the next medicine man for the village."

Bo's eyes changed colors from brown to grey, and his fangs became extended, and Shana fell back, hurriedly scooting away from him. "What was that?" She yelled. "Are you even a man?"

Bo changed back and said, "Yes, but you can't tell anyone about my abilities. I'm also part wolf."

Sunny said, "Well, we can see that, but I don't care. You are still my son and I still love you, even with your special abilities. I won't tell anyone and Shana and the medicine man won't tell anyone either. We can't tell anyone because the people in the village won't understand. You see how Shana just reacted; you scared the poor girl out of her skin."

Bo got up and knelt down by Shana and held her hand. She was shaking, and Bo pulled her close and held her and whispered in her ear, "It's me, Bo, and I would never hurt you."

Shana could feel his comfort. She also felt a tingling sensation all over her body, so she hugged Bo. "I know you won't hurt me. You just scared me, because I have never seen anything like that before, but I'm ok now."

They continued hugging, looking into each other's eyes for a long time, until Shana's father cleared his throat.

"You two were hugging a little bit too long," he said. "Now have a seat."

Sunny asked Bo how long he would be staying.

"I will be leaving in the morning. I came looking for information and, now that I have it, there is no other reason for me to stay. Plus the chief doesn't like me."

Shana's father nudged her to speak up; because he knew she wanted Bo to stay.

"But can't you stay a few days?" Shana asked, "So I can get to know you, and so I can teach you about the history of the village?"

Shana's father said, "You can even stay with us."

Sunny smiled. "I would like to get to know you, too."

Looking at all three of their expectant faces, Bo reconsidered. "Ok, I will stay about five days, but then I will leave because I have to get back home to my mother and father."

Sunny protested. "This is your home, and I am your mother and the chief is your father. We need you here."

"I can't stay," Bo said, "But I will keep coming back to visit you. I have been having dreams about you all my life, so now I hope they will stop. Somehow, I am connected to you just like I am connected to the wolves."

"You have talked enough," Shana chided Bo. "Now eat your food and you can stay with us because we have plenty of room. Bo agreed to stay with Shana and her father. Everyone finished eating and Bo decided to go for a walk, and he took Fang with him.

Sunny asked Bo to walk her home, and as everyone watched, Sunny held Bo's arm. Sunny was so proud to have Bo back in her life. When they got to her tent, Bo wouldn't enter. Sunny told him she would come and visit him in the morning.

Bo continued his evening walk with Fang, and all the teenage girls smiled and waved as Bo passed by.

Shana met Bo and asked him if she could walk with him, and he agreed. She held Bo's hand and pointed to the stars as they walked and talked. She asked Bo, "Are you planning on getting married?"

"No," he said. "I want to enjoy my life first. I want to spend as much time as I can with my father Jim Bo and my mother Cheyenne." He told her, "I also like to strip off all of my clothes and run naked with my brothers and sisters through the forest."

Shana laughed loudly. "You are joking!"

"I'm telling you the truth," Bo said.

Shana said, "WOW," that is so unbelievable. I would love to do something like that, but if I strip off all my clothes and run through the forest naked, I would have every boy in the village running behind me, trying to mate with me like some kind of wild animal. Sorry, I didn't mean to say that. I would like to get to know you better," Shana said.

"I would like that, too," Bo replied.

Chapter 5

Bo Stays Five Days in the Indian Village

The heart of all men dwells in the same wilderness.

Medicine man

The next day, after Bo's arrival, Sunny tried to go visit Bo, but Chief Running Bear didn't want her to. "He is my only son," she told him. "I missed watching him grow up because of you; I will not lose my only son again." She walked out of the tent and went to visit Bo. When she arrived, Shana told Sunny that Bo was still sleeping. Sunny said, "Then I will wait until he wakes up." She waited a while, as she helped Shana make breakfast. "I have seen how you look at my son, and I think the both of you will make a nice couple."

"Bo doesn't seem to have that kind of love in his heart," Shana said, "but yes, I do like him. If he isn't looking for love, however, then I won't pressure him. Bo just wants to be with his wolves, because that's all he talks about."

Sunny told Shana to give him time because he was not like the rest of them. "All he knows are his wolves. Please don't give up on him, but just give him some time to adjust to being around people." Bo finally woke up and joined them. Shana made him and Fang a plate of fish and bread cakes.

The village alarm was sounded, and everyone went outside. Bo said. "It's the wolves. Fang and I must go, but we will return."

"What about your food?" Shana asked.

"We will eat when we return," Bo said, hurrying away.

All the wolves were standing in the tree line when Bo and Fang walked outside. Everyone was afraid of the large pack of wolves, so Bo tried to calm them down. "It's ok. These are my brothers and sisters, and they won't harm anyone; they are just here to visit me. Bo and Fang walked up to greet the other wolves and they started running through the forest.

"Your son is strange," Shana told Sunny, "but I like him, and I can tell he has a good heart."

"I love him, too," Sunny replied. "It's hard to believe that he died in my arms and then returned to life and grew to be a strong, handsome, and brave young man. Maybe it wasn't time for him to die; maybe he was put here to protect the wolves."

Shana's father returned home, and he could see that Shana was very happy. He told her, "I have never seen you this excited before in all your life. It has to be Bo." Then he lifted a hand, as if warding off danger. "Shana, do not to get too attached to him, because he will not stay, and you will only get your heart broken. Bo is a man of the wilderness, and he is not ready to settle down. It seems to me that he is a man that was born to be wild. There are plenty of young men here in the village who would like to marry you and settle down. Why do you have to go after one that will not stay?"

"I am not going after Bo," Shana said.

But her father shook his head. "Your heart and the look on your face says something different. I have never seen you this happy before, and it only shows when you are around Bo."

"Enough. I will not listen to this type of talk," Shana said, and she walked out of the tent and went for a walk to clear her head.

Sunny told the medicine man, "I think we have a problem."

"Yes, I know," he replied. "I can see right into that girl's heart, and I see that it is going to be broken."

When Shana returned from her walk, Sunny was still there at the tent waiting on Bo to return.

The medicine man brought up the conversation again about Bo. "Why do you have to go after a boy who will not stay? He will only leave you in the end."

"Have you ever thought that maybe I would want to leave and go with him?" Shana replied. The medicine man just sat down, as if someone had put a knife through his heart.

Shana ran to her father and apologized and told him it was just a suggestion. But he asked, "Why would you want to leave here? These are your people and this is your home. You are next in line to be the village medicine woman. If you leave, they won't have medicine or anyone to care for them."

"It was only a suggestion," Shana said, again. "I don't plan on leaving my people. I need to continue my studies."

"Your heart speaks only the truth."

Bo and Fang returned from their run with the other wolves. Shana was happy to see him and her father just smiled and looked at Sunny. "He has only been gone for a few hours, and look at them."

"Let the kids have some fun," Sunny said.

Bo sat down to eat, and Shana sat down to talk to him. Sunny sat in the medicine man's rocking chair and admired Bo from a distance, because she was just happy to be in his presence.

Sunny asked Bo if his dreams had stopped and he said they had. "You were the key to my dreams, and now that I have met you, the dreams have stopped." Bo continued eating his food, and Shana asked Bo if they could go for a walk after he finished eating, and Bo agreed.

"We could go down by the river and relax," Shana said and smiled.

Shana's father put his hand on her shoulder and said, "Remember what we talked about."

"Can I come and visit you, Jim Bo, and Cheyenne at home one day?" Shana asked.

Bo smiled. "Sure, if it's ok with your father." After Bo finished eating, he and Shana walked down to the river, and Bo decided to go for a swim. Shana decided to get undressed and go swimming too. They swam for a long time and played in the water, while Fang just stayed on shore by the riverbank and watched them play and have fun.

As Shana and Bo played, Shana told Bo, "I like being your friend. I have never had this much fun in a very long time. I would like to be your friend forever."

Bo told Shana that forever was a very long time. As they continued to swim together and play in the water, Shana swam close to Bo and their eyes met and she kissed him. Bo pushed Shana away and explained that she shouldn't get too attached to him because he would be leaving in a few days.

"It's ok, because I will miss you, anyway," Shana said.

"We have different paths in life to follow," Bo told her.

But Shana told Bo how much she liked him and that maybe one day she could be his wife.

"Shana, don't talk like that. I'm not ready to be a husband yet."

Shana kissed Bo again and he kissed her back, then he decided to get out of the water.

"Did I do something wrong?" Shana asked.

"No, you didn't do anything wrong," Bo replied. "I am just not ready yet."

"I like you," Shana told Bo, "and I want to be close friends with you. I don't want you to go after any other girl in my village, because I think they all want you. And they are all looking for husbands."

"Shana, if you are looking for a husband, then you should just pick one of the boys in your village to be your husband."

"No, I want you," Shana said, "Because something in my heart tells me you are the right man for me."

"You know I have a special condition," Bo replied. "I am half wolf and I can't change that."

"I don't care about your condition, because all I see is a man with a good, caring heart."

Bo and Shana lay on the grass staring at the beautiful blue sky. They continued to talk for hours, and, as the sun began to go down, Bo said, "We should be going back to the village."

As they walked back, Shana held Bo's hand. Bo noticed that everyone was staring at them, when they walked into the village, and he asked Shana why everyone was staring.

Shana replied, "Because we are holding hands."

Bo said, "What's wrong with two people holding hands, walking and talking?"

"Some of the girls like you, and they want you just like I do. Some of the boys want me, but I don't want them. I want you."

"But we are just friends," Bo replied. "The people here in your village are strange."

"But this is your village, too," Shana replied. "You were born here."

"But I was not raised here," Bo said. "I am like a stranger here, and the chief doesn't even like me, and he is supposed to be my natural father."

"Have you ever thought that, since he is your father, you might grow up to be just like him?"

"No, I will never be like him, because I am like my other father, Jim Bo, and my mother Cheyenne. They are my true parents, and I love them both, and I won't turn my back on them. I won't ever abandon them. Although Sunny is my real mother and I am sorry for her loss, I must return home. I will come back and visit all the time, but I can't stay."

"I have a good idea," Shana said, "why don't you ask your mother Cheyenne and your father Jim Bo to move back to the village. They were born here, too. If they move back, then you could move back with them."

"I think my mother and father are happy living in the mountains," Bo said. "When I go home I will ask them. But it would be difficult, because all my parents are brothers and sisters, and my father Jim Bo was exiled from the village. I am the link between all of them. If they did move back to the village and things didn't work out between them, then I would have to leave the village and they would have to move back up into the mountains. I could not put them through all of that; it will be too painful for Cheyenne."

Bo and Shana finally arrived at her tent, still holding hands, and her father became angry and wanted to know what kind of relationship they had. The medicine man told Bo that if he wanted to be serious with Shana then he would have to marry her.

"We are not serious," Bo said. "We were just holding hands and talking. And I will not marry Shana. Are all of you people in this entire village crazy? Marriage is all everyone talks about," he said, upset. "That's it. I'm tired of all of this evil and rude behavior from everyone here. I will be packing my things and I will be leaving as soon as possible."

Shana started screaming and crying and begging Bo not to leave. Sunny also begged Bo not to leave.

Sunny explained that the medicine man didn't want him and Shana having sex without being properly married.

"We never had sex," Bo replied. "We're just friends, but everyone seems to keep accusing me of things I didn't do. I don't have these problems at home, so that's where I'll go. I will go back home." Bo packed all of his things and tied them to his horse. Shana came out of the tent crying, ashamed and embarrassed.

Shana hugged Bo and kissed him and begged him not to leave. "You have only been here two days, and you said you would stay here for five days."

Sunny walked up to Bo and hugged him, too. "You are a good son, but I understand your anger. I love you and I am going to miss you, but please don't forget about me and come and visit again soon."

Bo turned to Shana and stared in her eyes as tears flowed down her face. He hugged her and whispered in her ear, "If you ever want to find me, just travel south toward the mountain." Then Bo waved his hand and two wolves came out of the tree line. Bo asked Shana to let the wolves sniff her, so she knelt down and held out her hand and the two wolves sniffed her and licked her face, and then Sunny knelt down with the wolves, too.

Bo again told Shana, "If you ever want to find me, just travel south, and the wolves will find you and bring you to me. They will protect you. They told me they like you and they trust you," and with those words, Shana started smiling.

"I am missing you already," Shana said.

Bo climbed onto his horse and slowly rode away, waving goodbye to Shana and Sunny. Bo rode past the village chief and just stared at him as he rode past. The chief waved goodbye to Bo, but he did not wave back.

Shana and Sunny both stood together with tears running down their faces as they watched the young man of their dreams ride off into the sunset. Fang turned and looked at Shana and howled goodbye, as all the other wolves followed.

Shana then turned to her father. "How could you do this to me? How could you shame me like this? Look around at all the villagers looking at me and shaking their heads; the whole village is laughing at me."

Sunny just looked at the village medicine man and shook her head in disgust. Sunny held both of Shana's hands, looked her in the eyes, and said, "Don't worry, both of you have a future together. I can see marriage and little ones running around. Just give it time. I promise you, everything will work out just fine. I can feel it. He is my son, and I will not let him go that easily. Bo will just have to have two mothers because I am not going to let him go."

Chapter 6

Shana Goes Looking for Bo

There comes a time when every relationship
Is tested, and the true strength of the bond
Is determined

Shana 20

Shana waited a full year for Bo to return, but he never did. She was miserable and sad the whole year. Sunny's relationship with her husband was not so good, either, because she blamed him for treating Bo badly when he had visited. Deep down inside, Chief Running Bear missed Bo also; he just didn't show it.

Shana's father asked her to forget about Bo. "There are plenty of other young men in the village you could marry," he said.

Shana told her father, "It is because of you that Bo left the village. I don't want any other young man in the village. I want Bo. I have thought about him every single day since the day he left."

Shana's father got upset and said, "If you want Bo that bad, then why don't you go after him and marry him? That is, if he's not already married."

Shana ran out of the tent crying and went to Sunny's tent; Sunny asked her what was wrong when she arrived.

Shana told her she missed Bo so much that it was making her sick. She told Sunny how much she loved Bo and she was going to find him and she would not rest until she located him.

The village chief was in the tent with Sunny and, as Shana looked at him, he told her to go to Bo if that would make her feel better.

Sunny asked Shana when she was leaving, and she said, "Right now." So Sunny packed some food and they both headed south on foot to look for Bo.

"This is a very crazy trip that we're about to take," Sunny said, "With a little food and only the clothes on our backs. We don't even know where we're going."

"Bo once told me to travel south and find the wolves," Shana said, "and the wolves will take me to him. It's a big chance, but it's the only chance we have of finding him."

"Well, we will look for him together," Sunny said. "I know you love Bo. I knew since the first day you met him, but you need to give him some time."

"But it's been a whole year," Shana said. "How much time does he need?"

"Let's hope he's ready to give his heart to you," Sunny said.

The women continued their trip through the forest, traveling south. They were beginning to get thirsty and hungry. They decided to eat and rest. As they sat and talked, Sunny told Shana that Bo is supposed to be the next village chief.

"Bo is not interested in being the village's next chief," Shana said. "Bo likes running free with his wolves."

After they finished eating, they resumed their journey, admiring all the beauty of the forest and all of the different types of animals that were not located in the forest near the village.

Shana heard noises up in the tree and she looked up and saw it was a bobcat. Sunny pulled out her knife and Shana said, "No, Bo would not want you to hurt any of the animals in the forest." They continued walking as night fell, and the temperature started to drop, but they still had not found Bo.

"We are going to have to find a warm place to rest," Sunny said. They searched, but they couldn't find one, so they just lay down by some fallen trees and cuddled and held each other to keep warm. They fell asleep, but shortly, Shana heard a sound and she looked up and a wolf was standing over them, growling.

Shana stretched out her hand and Sunny said, "Are you crazy? You're going to get bit."

But Shana disagreed. "This is what Bo told me to do; he told me to trust the wolves. If they can identify me, they will take me to Bo. The wolf sniffed Shana's hand then sat down by her; she was cold and shaking. The wolf howled and all the wolves came out of the tree line and also lay near Shana and Sunny to keep them warm. A few wolves even lay on top of them.

"This is amazing," Sunny said, "How these wolves are trying to protect us."

"It's only because Bo asked them to protect us; we need to get our rest, because we don't know when the wolves will be ready to leave in the morning."

The next morning, the wolves were on the move, and Sunny and Shana followed them as they traveled along the tree line. The wolves traveled fast, so they had to keep back-tracking, because the women could not keep up. The women finally arrived at the forest clearing.

Cheyenne was picking some vegetables from the garden, and she could feel someone standing behind her; as she turned around, she saw Sunny standing there, not saying a word. She ran to her sister and embraced her, both of them crying.

Jim Bo came out of the tent and he stopped in his tracks. He could not believe his eyes when he saw Sunny hugging Cheyenne.

Bo could hear all the noise outside, so he went outside to see what all the noise was about. When Bo appeared, Shana saw him and ran to him and told him how much she had missed him. She kissed him, and he kissed her back, which surprised her. Bo told her how much he had missed her and how happy he was to see her.

Shana asked Bo why he had never returned to visit her. He explained that he could feel that he was not truly welcomed there, "So I decided not to return to your village. I missed you, though," Bo said.

"I missed you, too," Shana said. "That's why I came to visit. I hope things will be better between us."

Cheyenne said, "Who is this young lady kissing my Bo?"

Sunny said, "This is Shana, and she is in love with Bo. That's why we're here. Shana could not stand to be without Bo any longer. She is the medicine man's daughter, and even though she's supposed to train to take over from him, she couldn't stand to be away from Bo any longer, so we traveled here to visit Bo."

"Sunny, it's been over twenty years," Jim Bo said, "and you still look as beautiful as ever."

She thanked him, then she said, "I am here is to visit my son, Bo. I hope he has told you the stories about how he came to be. I told him part of the story about the blue fish in the river, and how he was placed in the river because everyone thought he was dead. We have a lot of making up to do," Sunny told Cheyenne. They continued to hold hands and talk.

Bo told his parents that he and Shana were going for a walk. They took Fang with them to the river.

Shana looked around and told Bo that the other wolves were following in the tree line.

"I know," Bo said. "They just like to stay out of sight."

Once they arrived at the river's shore, they lay down in the sand and talked. Shana explained how much she loved him, and Bo told Shana he understood because he had finally realized he loved her too.

"But what about your love for the wolves?" Shana asked.

"I love my wolves," Bo told her, "but I am human and I need a woman in my life, and I want you to be that woman."

Shana was elated. She asked, "How can we be together when we are so far apart? You live in the mountains, and you don't want to move to our village. I can't leave the village because I'm next in line to be the village medicine woman."

"Your father is the village medicine man right now, so you can stay here and live with me and my mother and father."

"I would like to stay, but I can't leave my father all alone," Shana said.

"We will work something out, Bo replied. "Let's not worry about these things right now." Instead, he asked Shana to go swimming. "We can even catch some fish for the wolf pack."

Shana smiled and said it would be fun.

Shana stripped off all of her clothes so she could entice Bo into making love to her.

Bo stared at her beautiful, naked body, but he did not make any sexual advances, and then he took off all of his clothes, too, and went into the water.

Shana followed Bo, and they played and wrestled in the water. Fang just lay on the riverbank and watched.

Bo and Shana started kissing and holding each other.

Shana stared into Bo's eyes and told him she loved him with all her heart. "I fell in love with you the first day I saw you. I knew you were the man for me, and I am glad you fell in love with me."

Then seeing that Bo was becoming interested, Shana told Bo, "Don't forget you have to feed Fang and the other wolves."

Bo sighed and asked her to help him catch some fish for them.

Shana was wondering how she was going to catch fish without any clothes on.

Bo caught the fish with his bare hands, but Shana wasn't having any luck, so Bo caught the fish and handed them to Shana. She threw the fish on shore so the wolves could feed. Fang grabbed the first fish and started eating. All the other wolves came out of the woods and ate as well. One of the wolves took Shana's clothes and ran off with them, but Bo howled, and the wolf brought the clothes back. After they fed all the wolves, Shana came out of the water naked, and some of the wolves gathered around her as she got dressed. Shana petted some of the wolves.

Bo told Shana that she had been accepted into the wolf clan.

Shana didn't realize that she had part of the gene that caused her to be accepted by the wolf pack. She didn't know and Bo didn't know, but the wolves could sense Shana had the wolf gene. She also didn't know that it made her the perfect mate for Bo. Fang didn't go near Shana while the other wolves were near her.

Bo finally came out of the water, and Fang ran to him, as all the other wolves started to leave and go back into the forest.

Bo asked Shana if she was ready to go back to his camp, but she said no, she wanted to stay at the river and spend some more time with him and relax.

Bo said they could stay, "but let's find a different spot, because the wolves have fed on this one."

They walked farther down the river, holding hands, until they found a clean area. They lay down in the sand and talked. Shana rolled over and kissed Bo, and he kissed her back. They enjoyed their time together. They stayed near the riverbank and watched the sunset come to an end before they started back to the camp.

"Shana, how long are you going to stay?" Bo asked

"As long as your mother Sunny stays," Shana said.

"I've enjoyed your visit. You don't know how I've longed to hold you in my arms."

She just smiled and knew Bo was now hers and that she had finally melted his heart. As they finally arrived back home, Cheyenne said, "Here comes our future; they're in love."

Shana looked at Sunny and winked. "Thank you for telling me to come after him, because he told me he loves me."

Sunny asked them if they had a good time.

Shana said, "Yes, but Bo still won't ask me too marry him."

Bo's eyes widened, surprised that Shana was thinking about marriage.

Cheyenne asked Bo about her grandkids and Bo said, "Wait, everybody needs to slow down, because I'm not ready for any of these things yet."

"Do you plan on staying young forever?" Cheyenne asked. "You need to start everything while you're still young."

"I'm ready," Shana replied, "but Bo isn't, so I'm not going to try to force him. I'll be patient until he is ready, because I don't want to argue over little things. I have waited a long time to get him, and I don't want to lose him, now."

Everyone sat down to eat dinner. Sunny was trying to get Cheyenne and Jim Bo to move back to the Indian village.

Jim Bo said, "There's no way we're moving back there; this is our home."

She asked Cheyenne and Jim Bo to think about Bo and his relationship with Shana. She explained how she was only trying to bring Shana and Bo together.

Cheyenne said, "If they are destined to be together, then it has to come naturally, and no one should interfere."

Bo told his parents, "No one should be trying to plan our lives for us, because I don't want to get married, I don't want to have any children, and I don't want to move to the Indian village just to be with Shana. Her father is rude and the village chief is rude. I don't want to be around rude people."

Jim Bo told everyone to just eat and let the kid plan his own future. So, after dinner, Bo and Shana stayed out late, talking and cuddling. They looked at the full moon so long that Cheyenne had to get out of bed to tell Bo and Shana to go to bed, and she made sure they both slept in separate beds.

The next morning, Bo left the tent early with Fang; Shana stopped him at the door and asked him where he was going, and he told her he was going running with his brothers and sisters.

Shana asked him what brothers and sisters, and he pointed outside. Shana saw all the wolves from the pack waiting for Bo and Fang.

Bo kissed Shana on the cheek and went running naked through the forest with the wolves.

Sunny asked Shana what was wrong, and she said nothing. "I was just talking to Bo, and he went running with his so-called brothers and sisters."

"Never let Bo hear you say anything bad about those wolves," Cheyenne told Shana, "Because he loves them; he was raised with them."

Jim Bo told Shana, "Please don't ever try to force Bo to choose between you and those wolves, because you will lose. He'll choose those wolves over you. Please give him some breathing room to run with them."

"We need to start thinking about building a huge log cabin, Cheyenne told Jim Bo, "because we need a larger place to live, and we need more room just in case we keep getting more visitors."

Chapter 7

Bo is severely injured

I will face my fear; I will permit it to pass
Through me, I am not afraid of death.

Bo 21

It had been a long hot day, and so as night fell, everyone was tired. Everyone decided to turn in for the night. Shana decided to stay outside just a little while longer as she enjoyed the nightly summer breeze.

Bo decided to go inside to get some blankets when Fang started to growl and ran outside.

Shana screamed and everyone ran outside and saw a big grizzly bear approaching her. Bo put himself between Shana and the bear and told Shana to run.

Fang started howling, so the other wolves would come and help, but they were too far away. The wolf pack heard Fang, and they ran toward the camp. Bo couldn't stop the grizzly bear, and he told Jim Bo that something was wrong with the bear, because he couldn't talk to it.

Bo told Fang to protect Shana, but Fang wouldn't listen, because he wanted to protect Bo.

Bo once again told Fang to protect Shana, so Fang took a protective stance in front of her. She was terrified and couldn't move. Bo didn't have any weapons and the grizzly charged toward him, and Fang once again charged the grizzly bear to protect Bo.

Fang charged the grizzly from the rear, and it gave Bo enough time to get Shana off the ground to safety. Jim Bo, Sunny, and Cheyenne then ran for cover.

But Shana refused to leave Bo, so she ran into the tent and grabbed two of Bo's knives and ran back to him and gave them to him, but Bo still refused to hurt the bear, so he turned into half wolf, and his eyes turned grey, and his fangs came down. "Why won't you talk to me?" Bo asked the bear.

Bo asked Shana to leave, but the bear charged Shana again, and Bo put himself between the bear and Shana again as she ran away. Fang tried to attack the bear from the rear, but the bear turned and slapped Fang with his huge claws, injuring Fang, when he was on the ground, trying to get up; the bear was intent on killing Fang, just as the wolf pack arrived. They all attacked the bear, and he continued to slap the wolves through the air. Many wolves lay on the ground hurt, but others continued to charge the grizzly.

Bo had no choice but to attack the grizzly to stop him; otherwise, he would kill all of Bo's wolves. Then a cougar and Bo's white horse arrived to help, but Bo knew they were no match for the grizzly, either, and he didn't want them to get hurt, so he waved his hand and asked them to back away. But they refused and ran beside Bo to protect him. Bo shoved both the cougar and the horse and told them to go. "It is too dangerous my brothers." And both the cougar and the horse slowly moved away, easing toward the tree line, still hissing. All the wolves began howling, and Bo dropped both of his knives and stood in front of the grizzly. "I will not harm you, so if you want to take my life, take it, and I will not resist."

Shana screamed, and as his parents watched in horror, the grizzly bear bit down on Bo's chest. Bo didn't scream; he just looked the bear in his eyes. The grizzly calmed down and released the badly injured Bo. The diseased grizzly was unharmed, but Bo lay badly injured on the ground. The wolves all around him were badly injured, as other wolves gathered around Bo.

Shana ran to Bo and held him in her arms, begging him not to die.

"That was dumb, what you did," Jim Bo said.

"It was the only way I could reach him, and it worked. I am badly injured but I will heal."

Sunny held one of Bo's hands and Cheyenne held the other, as they both cried.

"I will take him into the tent," Jim Bo said.

Shana said, "I have been learning about medicines and I will treat him." All three women cried half the night while looking after Bo. Fang was injured, so Jim Bo patched him up and Fang stayed by Bo's side. All the other wolves outside refused to leave; they stayed in the tree line.

The grizzly never returned. Shana treated Bo's injuries, but he was in a lot of pain. She had to go into the forest to get herbs, and Jim Bo decided to go with her to protect her. A few of the wolves followed Shana and Jim Bo as they looked for medicine.

"Bo is hurt very badly," Shana told Jim Bo, "and if I can't help him, I will have to ride to the village and get my father."

"Bo is a very strong young man," Jim Bo told her. "We will all take turns watching over him."

"I really want to marry Bo," Shana admitted, "and have his kids."

"I already know, because I have seen how you look at him," Jim Bo said. "It is nothing but pure love. I wish you both the best of luck." They searched the forest for a few hours looking for herbs.

Shana collected a lot of herbs, so she wouldn't have to come back looking for more. They returned to the campsite and Shana prepared the herbs for Bo's wounds, and Cheyenne helped her.

Cheyenne told Shana, "You will be a good wife for Bo, and I am proud of you. Jim Bo and I both approve of your relationship with Bo, so please push as hard as you have to if you want to keep him, because, sometimes, Bo can be a little stubborn. Please don't let any other woman have him; we want you to have him. When he recovers, I will have a talk with him," Cheyenne said.

"Is there anything else we can do for Bo?" Sunny asked. "I don't want my only boy to die."

Jim Bo said, "Maybe we all should get some rest. We can take turns watching over him. You all can get some rest; I'll be happy to watch over him."

Cheyenne told Jim Bo, "This attack gives us even more reason to build a log cabin. If we had a log cabin, we all could have run inside and closed the door and we would have been protected from the bear."

Cheyenne told him, "I am not blaming you or anyone. I just want us to be safe next time.

Jim Bo agreed. "When Bo gets better, I will build us a large log cabin. I will do anything to keep you happy. The way things look; Shana and Bo will probably be having kids real soon."

Shana dressed Bo's wounds and gave him a pain killer solution to drink; then everyone went to bed and Shana climbed in bed beside Bo.

Bo was bedridden for a few weeks because of the pain, and his wounds were not healing, and everyone began to worry about Bo's health. Fang never left Bo's side, and all the other wolves were outside the camp.

Shana was crying as she walked out of the tent. She told everyone that Bo was not getting any better and she was beginning to worry. She told them she couldn't heal him and that she must go get her father from the village.

"No, I will go," Sunny said, "because I also miss my husband."

"You don't know the way back, plus you can't travel alone, so I will go with you," Cheyenne said. "I know the way. My husband has been exiled from the village but I have not. We will go and bring the medicine man back."

"Please go and hurry back with him," Jim Bo said. "Shana and I will take care of Bo. I will also start working on building you a new log cabin."

Cheyenne packed food for the trip.

Shana told everyone, "I will go and get more herbs for Bo's wounds."

Jim Bo told Shana to take Fang with her, but she refused. "Please let Fang stay with Bo. I will be ok; I'm sure the other wolves will follow and protect me. As she walked toward the forest, some of the wolves followed her, and Shana said, "See what I'm talking about?" Shana did not know she had been born with the wolf gene, but her genes weren't as strong as Bo's; still, the wolves could sense her.

Sunny and Cheyenne mounted Bo's white horse with a few supplies and rode north toward the Indian village. Jim Bo went back into the tent after seeing them off.

Shana arrived with more medicine as Bo woke up in pain and tried to get out of bed.

Jim Bo told him to stay in bed, and he told Shana he would be gone for a few hours and to keep a close eye on Bo; then he went to the river to get some fish.

Bo told Shana she looked as beautiful as ever. "I had a dream that we were married and had two children."

Shana started crying and said, "I would be glad to have your children, any day," as he wiped away her tears.

"What do you wish for right at this moment?" Bo asked

Shana said, "I would like to make love to you so I can have your child."

"I would love to, as well, but I don't have the strength," Bo said.

Shana said, "I could do all the work. Your father said he would be down at the river for a few hours getting dinner. You just stay still so you won't reopen your wounds."

Bo lay down exhausted from his injuries. Shana took off her clothes and climbed on top of Bo, being careful not to reopen the wounds in his chest. She looked him in his eyes as she slowly made love to him, while she told him how much she loved him and told him to give her a baby. Bo said, "The rest is up to the gods, and if it is meant to be, then you will have my baby." Fang just lay quietly on the floor while Shana and Bo made love. They both climaxed at the same time, and Shana trembled with ecstasy and collapsed on top of Bo. "I love you," she whispered in his ear.

Once they finished making love, all the wolves outside the tent moved in closer and surrounded the tent. Shana got dressed and lay back down next to Bo and held him gently. Bo was still weak when his father returned with dinner.

Shana got up from the bed and told Jim Bo she would cook dinner, but she had to clean up and wash herself first. Shana went outside and bathed as the wolves watched. She returned and prepared their dinner.

Jim Bo said, "I can't stand to see Bo like that. Tomorrow I will start building the new log cabin."

Shana fed Bo and then ate dinner herself. After that, everyone went to bed.

Bo told Shana that, after making love to her, he was beginning to feel better.

Shana told him to just rest and get some sleep.

The next morning, Bo was awake, but he stayed in bed as Shana woke up. Bo told her he was feeling better. He was recovering from his injuries; they tried to figure out what had suddenly caused him to start recovering.

Shana said, "It wasn't the wolves, because they' always stay outside. The only thing left is that we made love, so maybe that caused you to start healing, but I don't know why."

Sunny and Cheyenne finally arrived at the Indian village. They ran straight to the medicine man's tent. The first thing he asked was where Shana was, and Cheyenne told him, "She is still at my home up in the mountains."

Sunny told the medicine man that Bo had been injured by a grizzly bear and he needed some help.

"How is that possible?" the medicine man replied. "I thought he could talk to the animals."

Cheyenne said, "We need you to come up to the mountains to treat his injuries."

The Indian chief came into the tent and hugged Sunny and said, "I really missed you. How was your trip?"

"It was awful," she replied, telling him that Bo had been hurt, mauled by a grizzly bear. "That's why we are here to get the medicine man."

The medicine man said, "Why didn't you bring him with you?"

"He was too badly hurt, and we couldn't move him," Sunny said.

The medicine man grabbed some of his medicines and potions and stuffed them into his bag. "Then we need to leave right away."

"Are you leaving again?" the chief asked Sunny, and she said, "Yes, he is our son."

"Sunny, do you want me to go with you?" the chief asked.

"No, you do what you do best and stay here. I will be back in a few days."

With that, Sunny, Cheyenne, and the medicine man went back up into the mountains. When they arrived, Jim Bo was outside setting up the foundation for the new log cabin.

Cheyenne asked Jim Bo how Bo was feeling, and he told her Bo was inside the tent. "He started recovering very fast, although I don't know why, but he still needs a lot of rest."

The medicine man, Sunny, and Cheyenne entered the tent, and Cheyenne ran to Bo.

Shana's father asked her how Bo was feeling, and she told him Bo was doing much better and healing very fast.

He then asked her how she was feeling, and she told him she was happy to be with Bo. Then he asked her when she was coming home, and she said, "I will be home in a few days."

The medicine man examined Bo, then looked at everyone. "How could Bo have been near death a few days ago? He is almost completely healed." The medicine man was trying to figure out how this was even possible. He told everyone he would stay a few days to make sure Bo was ok, then he would return to the village.

Jim Bo thanked the medicine man for coming. The medicine man told Bo he was glad he was all right, because he only wanted Shana to be happy. "As long as Shana is with you, she is always happy. The medicine man saw all the wolves surrounding the camp. "Is it safe with all these wolves just hanging around?"

Shana said, "Yes, they are Bo's brothers and sisters."

The medicine man said, "I don't understand what you are talking about, and I really don't want to know, because it sounds a little crazy to me."

Everyone went outside to enjoy the night, but Shana stayed inside with Bo as he rested.

Bo told Shana how much he loved her and how grateful he was for her looking after him and his injuries.

All the adults were outside talking, and Jim Bo asked the medicine man if Bo could have Shana's hand in marriage if he ever decided to ask her. "We don't want to force them into anything they don't want to do."

"I think they make a perfect couple," Sunny said.

"They are very much in love," Cheyenne said. "The only problem we have is the half-breed problem Bo has," Sunny said. "But that's my fault; many years ago, I ate the blue fish from the river, which caused devastation to our village. We lost nineteen newborn babies that year."

"I have tried to keep Shana and Bo apart for a specific reason," the medicine man said, "but all I've done is cause a rift between me and my daughter. So, I must reveal a long-kept secret. Shana might be the product of the blue fish syndrome, too."

"That is impossible," Sunny said. "Shana was born a year after the river incident. My husband forbade any more eating of the fish from the river for a whole year, and times were hard. There was no food, and we nearly starved the village out of existence."

"I have a confession to make," the medicine man said. "My wife and I had stored some dried blue fish that year, and we ate it, so we wouldn't starve. We didn't truly believe the blue river fish was the cause of all the babies' deaths. The only clue we had was that all the babies were born with blue skin. My wife only ate small pieces of the fish, so we could make it last. Eventually, we still ran out of food. Later, we found out my wife was with child. We kept the fish subject a secret. My wife died giving birth to Shana, and she was not blue when she was born."

"That explains why the wolves are so protective of her; they know Shana is one of them, just like Bo," Sunny said. "Has anyone else noticed how the wolves follow her around and protects her?"

"Yes," everyone replied, "it's like Bo and Shana were destined for each other."

"We must not tell them; we must let nature take its course," the medicine man said, and everyone agreed.

Chapter 8

Shana Realizes She is With Child

When the true motive is love, there is
No other explanation. Searching for love
Is like chasing grains of sand in the wind.

Shana 20

Bo recovered from his injuries and Shana, Sunny, and the medicine man prepared to return home to their Indian village. Bo was strong enough to help his father Jim Bo build their new log cabin.

Shana went for a walk with Cheyenne, and they discussed Shana and Bo's future.

Shana told Cheyenne that Bo was not ready for a family yet, but that when he was ready, then she would return. "But I will visit Bo, and he can come visit me," she told Cheyenne.

Cheyenne and Shana continued to walk along the river shoreline. "I feel like we are being watched," Cheyenne said.

"We are," Shana said. "It's the wolves. Some of them always follow me wherever I go. I don't understand them, but maybe Bo asked them to look after me."

"Maybe there is some kind of connection between you, Bo, and wolves," Cheyenne suggested.

"I am going to be honest with you," Shana said. "Bo and I made love while you and Sunny were away."

"That was not a wise idea," Cheyenne said, "because you could have gotten pregnant, and your father would be upset, because you are not married and because Bo is not ready for a family yet."

"I want to have Bo's baby, because I think it was meant to be," Shana said in return.

Cheyenne didn't respond, because she didn't want to reveal to Shana about her being part wolf with the genetic gene.

"If I do become pregnant, I will stay away and have the baby on my own, so I won't disturb Bo."

"That is not a good idea, either," Cheyenne said. "You will be denying Bo the right to see his baby. And that would only cause more problems, because he might think the baby is not his. This is a problem you will have to solve on your own."

Shana and Cheyenne returned to the camp. Sunny was cooking lunch for everyone. Bo walked over to Shana and gave her a hug and a kiss. Shana told Bo, "I've decided to leave in the morning. I will be going back to my village. I will come and visit you sometimes before winter comes."

The next day, Bo said goodbye to Shana, Sunny, and the medicine man. When they departed, the wolves did not follow them. Bo asked Cheyenne why she was crying and she told him, "because Sunny is my sister and I will miss her."

"You can always visit her in the village, and I will go with you, because I would like to visit Shana." After some time had passed, Bo returned to helping Jim Bo build their new log cabin. As the days went on, Bo got stronger, and the new home was getting close to completion. Cheyenne just stood back and looked at the new log cabin and smiled. She was thinking *if only we would have had the log cabin earlier, maybe Bo wouldn't have gotten hurt*. She tried to put the tragedy behind her. The wolves came every day, so Bo could run with them, but Bo refused, because he wanted to spend more time with Cheyenne and Jim Bo. So, since Bo didn't go with the wolves, they came to visit him.

All the wolves came to visit him, and they brought all their pups. Cheyenne played with the puppies. She told Bo that something was wrong. "Why are all the wolves coming to the camp?"

Bo explained that they missed him and visiting was their way of showing him that they needed him with the wolf pack.

But Jim Bo told Bo to look around, because the wolves were trying to send him a message.

"I understand," Bo said. "Once we finish the cabin, I will start spending more time with them." Some of the puppies wobbled over to him and he picked them up and kissed them. "I haven't forgotten about you guys," he told them. "I just need some time to rest."

Bo constantly thought about Shana and he missed her being around, and he also missed her soft voice and soft touch. Bo realized that the only way he could get over missing Shana was to get on with his life and stay busy.

Cheyenne saw Bo working very hard helping his father on the log cabin. She asked both of them to take a break.

Bo sat down to eat, and he looked into Cheyenne's eyes. "Mom, you know I can see things, so do you want to tell me and dad what is wrong?"

She replied, "I'm just worried about everything that has been happening, and I miss Shana and Sunny."

"You will see them again," Bo said, "and when dad finishes building the new five bedroom cabin, it will be big enough for everyone to rest comfortably."

Jim Bo told Cheyenne that the new log cabin was almost finished.

The next day Bo went outside and stared at the wolves then took off his clothes and decided to be their leader again. As he started to run, the wolves took off one at a time traveling behind Bo; they ran for miles, and Bo remembered the good times they used to have. Bo stopped and arched his chest and howled as loudly as he could to clear his lungs, and he frightened nearly every animal in the forest for miles around. All the other wolves started howling as well, to show their strength. Bo took off running again with the wolves close behind. He finally realized they were very far from home, so he thought it was time they started heading back home; he wasn't even tired, but he was worried about the other wolves. He reduced his running speed on the way back, because he knew the wolves were tired and exhausted. While they ran, Bo came across the bear that had attacked him; the bear was near death.

Bo told the other wolves to stay back, approaching the bear and looking into his eyes.

The bear told Bo he was sorry for attacking him.

Bo told the bear his apologies were accepted and that he knew the bear was ill, which was why he refused to kill him.

Bo told the bear to go ahead and die in peace, and the bear grunted and took his last breath and died. The wolves again tried to approach, but Bo told them to stay away because of the disease the bear carried. Bo dug a big hole and buried the grizzly bear to keep the disease from spreading, because he knew the other wild animals in the forest would try to eat the dead bear. After Bo buried the bear, he and the other wolves continued their journey home. Bo again stopped and took a dip in the river, because he had touched the grizzly bear. He then continued running and decided he would let Shana go and he would remain with his brothers and sisters.

Cheyenne and Jim Bo were back at the camp, and Cheyenne asked Jim Bo if he was up to building another log cabin.

"Why, what do you have in mind?" he asked.

"If Bo and Shana decide to get married or just live together, they will need their own home."

"They already said they were not ready to settle down," Jim Bo said.

"I had a long talk with Shana the other day," Cheyenne said, "and she is very much in love with Bo; she doesn't want to lose him. I promised her she was welcome back here anytime, and I told her if she wants Bo, she has to push him a little, but not too hard. I know Bo loves her, but he is torn between her and the wolves. I don't want to move back to the village, because this is our home. I don't want Bo to move there either, nor do I want to take Shana away from her home, and this is why there is a problem between Bo and Shana. Bo doesn't want to leave his wolves, and Shana doesn't want to leave the village."

"I have an idea, then," Jim Bo said. "How about if we build Bo and Shana a log cabin somewhere between here and the village Bo can run with his wolves and Shana can live near the village, and that way everyone is happy."

"That is a good idea," Cheyenne said, "But we will wait to see what Shana and Bo do first, because we don't need to interfere in their lives. There is enough pain between those two already."

* * *

In the Indian village, Sunny was crying because she missed Bo so much.

Her husband said, "If you miss him so much, then you need to go to him. I know I made a mistake in the beginning by putting him in the river, but that is in the past, and there is nothing I can do about it now. I won't try to stop you from loving your own son. I miss him, too, and I promise the next time I see him; I will sit down and talk to him. I will try to work things out with him."

Sunny thanked her husband and said, "Please at least try. I know neither of you see eye to eye, but Bo tried in the beginning to talk to you, and you accused him of making love to me, not knowing he was our son; then you started a fight with him. I understand your jealousy and anger, but we almost lost our only son to that grizzly bear. I want to spend some time with Bo and get to know him, because he is our only son, and you should get to know him too."

The chief said, "I will do my best to get to know Bo better."

"I will try not to go to Bo. I will let Bo come to us," Sunny said. "Bo is a very private person, and he loves his wolves. He even loves them more than Shana."

Shana was enjoying some quiet time with her female friends, and some young Indian men came around. One of the young men asked Shana out, but she said no. Then the young man tried to kiss her, and she slapped his face and told him, "Don't you ever try that again, and that goes for all of you men here. I'm in love with Bo," Shana said.

"You mean to tell me you chose mountain boy over your own people."

"No, I chose him, because he is one of our people and he is special. Bo was born in this village; just because he doesn't choose to live here doesn't make him an outcast."

"Anyone who runs with wolves is a savage," the young man said.

"You're wrong. Bo is smart and gentle; you need to get to know him before you can judge him. Bo is the man for me, and I will wait for him, until he says otherwise," Shana said. Shana told everyone, "Bo is the chief's son. And his mother is Sunny, so that makes Bo a member of this village."

All of her friends told her that, if she didn't want Bo, they would like to have him.

Shana told them no, that she would like to marry him. All the young men got upset and left the group. All the young women stayed to talk to Shana to hear about the adventures she had when she went to visit Bo.

Shana told them about Bo and the wolves and the grizzly bear attack. She also told them about how the wolves followed her around and accepted her into their clan. She never told them about how she made love to Bo, because she wanted everything to stay a secret.

The next morning Shana was feeling sick, so she went out for a walk down to the river to get some water. She sat down to take a break, and she heard a sound in the woods. As she turned around, she saw six wolves. She thought Bo was with them but he was not; it was only the wolves passing by the village.

Shana asked the wolves to come to her and they did. She hugged and kissed them, and they were happy to see her. She stayed at the river bank for hours with the wolves. The sun started to go down, so Shana had to go home, and the wolves walked her to the edge of the forest.

Shana told the wolves to go home but to come back and visit her soon, because she missed them. She left the forest, and when she got to the tent, her father was waiting for her.

He asked her where she had been.

"I was down at the riverbank."

He said, "I don't believe you, because you have been gone all day."

"If you must know," Shana replied, "I was with six visiting wolves and I miss them. I don't have to explain myself to you."

"Why?" her father asked, "Because you were with Bo?"

"No," Shana said, "It was only the wolves that were passing through. They were happy to see me, so I'm sure they'll be back." Shana suddenly pushed away from her father and threw up her lunch.

"How long have you been sick," he asked.

"About a month," she said.

"Are your breasts sore?"

Shana admitted that they were.

"Did you make love to anyone?" the medicine man then asked.

Shana admitted that she had. "To Bo," she said.

"Are you sure it was Bo and only Bo?"

"Yes, why?"

"Poor girl, you have just gotten yourself into a very big problem, and it is something you will have to deal with on your own. I will not say another word. You are with child, and it's Bo's child. So I guarantee you, the wolves will be back. You must contact Bo and tell him."

"No," Shana said, "Unless he comes to visit, he must not know. Bo needs to clear his mind of all the troubles that's bothering him."

Then Shana said, "You must keep my pregnancy a secret," and he agreed.

"I will keep your secret," her father said, "but your stomach will start to swell and everyone is going too eventually know you are pregnant."

"Then I will go to the river every morning to meet the wolves, so I can keep them away from the village, and you can go with me if you don't trust me."

"I trust you, but I am worried about your future, because your mother died in child birth, and I don't want to lose you, too." The medicine man gave her some medicine for her morning sickness. He asked her if she was going to see Bo and she said no.

Shana told him that she would not tell Sunny about her pregnancy, and when her stomach started to swell and everyone found out she was pregnant she would tell everyone she was pregnant by someone else, as the rumors would spread like a wildfire. Shana took some herbal medicine and lay down in bed to get some rest. Sunny stopped by for a visit, but Shana's father told her Shana was resting because she was not feeling well.

Chapter 9

Rumors

Evil does not have a face,
Nor does it have a soul.

Medicine man

Shana started spending all her time at the riverbank, and every day she would go there to meet the wolves. She went to the river one day but the wolves were not there yet, so she decided to wait for them. Shana lay down and closed her eyes and thought about how much she missed Bo. The Indian boy Rulan, who liked Shana, had followed her to the river to see where she was going every day and decided to hide in the bushes and watch her. Shana was resting with her eyes closed, and when she opened her eyes, the young man was standing over her. Shana did not panic. She asked, "What do you want, pest?"

"I followed you here, so I could spend some time with you," he said.

"I don't want to spend the day with you," Shana said, "Because I hate you, because you are rude and you tell lies all the time. You tell lies most when you're around all your friends. I don't want you spreading rumors around about me about how we spend the day together and have sex."

Rulan said, "I always liked you, ever since we were kids."

"Well, I've grown up, but I don't know about you," Shana said. "So I'm asking you again to leave."

"Not until I get what I came for," he said. "I want to have sex with you and I want to marry you."

"We are not having sex, and I will not marry you," Shana said.

Rulan suddenly grabbed Shana and climbed on top of her. They struggled as he tried to remove her clothes. He quickly ripped off her top, revealing her breasts.

"You have very nice breasts," he panted in lust. They struggled, as he tried to remove her pants. He tried to rape Shana, but she continued to fight him off.

She fought him until her last breath, with all her strength, until she was completely exhausted. She stopped struggling, and he continued to take off her clothes Shana cried and said, "Please don't do this to me," but the young Indian boy just laughed and said, "I knew I would have my way with you; so you finally give up. Just get ready, because you are going to enjoy this, whether you like it or not."

Shana continued to cry as she tried once again to push him away. She screamed, "Somebody please help me!" With one last effort, she forced herself to let out a roar and, to her surprise, she howled like a wolf.

The Indian boy said, "I think you have been hanging around mountain boy too long, because you are beginning to think you are a wolf."

He smiled and leaned down to kiss Shana, and she smiled back. "I knew you would come around," he said, "Now, just relax. This will be over before you know it. But before he could look up, six wolves were standing around him growling, inches from his face. He jumped off of Shana and tried to crawl away.

The wolves circled him and Shana said, "Now it's time for you to beg for your life." She collected her clothes and started putting them back on. "Beg for your life," she said. "Otherwise, my friends are going to rip you to pieces."

The young man started begging and apologizing. But Shana laughed. "Now you see how it feels to fear for your life. Shana continued laughing. Look at you sniveling on the ground just like the coward you are. I will report this to the chief and my father and let them deal with you." Shana told the wolves to let him go, because if they attacked him, there would be a war hunt for all the wolves. Shana finished dressing and went home and told her father what had happened and they went to see Chief Running Bear.

But Rulan had already gone to see the chief with his parents and told him a lie that he and Shana were having sex and Shana changed her mind, because she was afraid her father would find out and get upset.

Rulan said, "She even said she was going to try to say I raped her and everyone would believe her and not me."

When Shana and her father arrived at the chief and Sunny's tent, they were very upset that the rumors had already started spreading. Shana and her father tried to explain to the chief and Sunny that the young Indian boy tried to rape Shana, and no one would believe them, and everyone looked at Shana like she was nasty.

Rulan's mother even spit in Shana's face and said, "You will never marry my son. You are not good enough to be part of our family."

The chief said, "If he tried to rape you, then why don't I see any bruises? Who else was there, and why was there no struggle. If he really tried to rape you why did you let him finish?"

The chief said, "I am sorry, but I don't believe you, because your story just doesn't make any sense. Shana realized that the young boy had once again told another perfect lie. But she couldn't tell them about the wolves and how she made him beg for his life.

Shana asked the young Rulan, "Were you just simply born a liar? Why won't you ever tell the truth about anything? One day, your lies are going to cost you your life, or it's going to cause you to be lonely and all alone, because no one is ever going to want you."

Sunny slapped Shana's face and told her, "I am ashamed of you. How could you do this to Bo?"

"So, you're going to take his word over mine?"

"Your story just doesn't make any sense," Sunny replied.

Shana said, "It's ok, because I don't care if no one believes me or not. Everyone please just keep on believing the liar over there."

Shana said, "One day, everyone will find out the truth, and I will not forgive either of you." Sunny and the chief just looked at each other astounded, trying to understand what Shana was talking about. The chief said, "This is what I mean; the girl is not making any sense."

"I will be sure to make both of you regret this day," Shana said. Then Shana turned to Sunny. "I thought you were my friend; you were just trying to use me to get close to Bo. I thought I could trust you, but I now see that you're just like the rest of the village idiots. I promise you, I will have the last laugh," Shana said.

The chief said, "Shana, you better be more worried about everyone in the village calling you the village whore."

"Everyone here won't have to worry about me, because I've just decided that, when the time comes, I will leave this village, because I know who my friends are."

The chief said, "That is enough. Now everyone get out of my tent and go home."

As Shana and her father left the tent, Shana told her father, "I swear to you, father, what I told you is the truth."

He said, "I know, Shana, and I believe you, but who saved you from being raped?"

"It was the wolves," Shana said, "But I couldn't tell them because they would try to make an excuse to hunt the wolves or try to say they are a danger to the village. Since no one will believe me, I will start inviting the wolves to the village to protect me, so there won't be any more chances of that bastard coming near me. He is a chronic liar and they believed him. The wolves will stay with us. Father, I swear to you, I am carrying Bo's baby. I have never been with anyone else except Bo. Once my baby is born, the chief and Sunny cannot come near my baby, even if they are the grandparents. I will make them pay for turning against me."

The medicine man said, "Shana, revenge is not the answer. You are only going to make the problems worse; let time work all the problems out."

Shana went home and cried half the night. Hearing her, her father got out of bed and told Shana, "You will have to learn to be strong," and they talked into the night.

The next morning, Shana got out of bed and her father was already outside. "Where are you going?"

"I'm going down to the river, and I would like for you to go with me. I want you to see the wolves for yourself, so there will be no doubt in your mind that I have told you the truth about everything I said." So Shana and her father walked down to the river. The wolves were already there this time. They greeted Shana, frolicking about and licking her face. Shana's father couldn't believe his eyes and how happy the wolves were to see her.

"I apologize, Shana, for all the times I doubted your stories; now I believe you." They stayed with the wolves for a few hours then the medicine man said, "We need to get back home."

"Good," Shana said, "Because I'm taking the wolves with me." When Shana and her father arrived back at the village with the wolves, everyone was watching and staring as they walked into their tent with the wolves. Shana's father told her, "The wolves can't stay in the tent because they are wild animals."

Shana said, "I know; they're free to come and go as they please. I just want them for protection, so there are no more attacks or accusations about who I'm sleeping with. When the time comes, I will go and visit Bo, Cheyenne, and Jim Bo."

He said, "I understand, and I will be losing you forever. The village will not only be losing a member, but they will also be losing their next medicine man."

"The winter season will be arriving, soon," Shana said, "so as long as I stay wrapped up with a heavy winter fur, no one will ever know I am pregnant."

The next day, the word reached the chief that there were wolves in the village, and the chief went to visit Shana.

He told Shana she had to get rid of the wolves because they were a danger to everyone in the village.

Shana stood defiantly. "No they are not. They are here for my protection from the rapist. The wolves are my friends and they are my responsibility. I will keep an eye on them, and everywhere I go, I will take them with me. I don't want to be a problem here, and in the spring, I'm planning on leaving your village."

"Where will you go?" the chief asked

"I don't know, maybe somewhere I can be happy and alone."

The chief said, "You are welcome to stay here, because this is your home. But if you want to leave to be with the wolves, then I won't try to stop you." The chief looked at the medicine man, and he told the chief. "It is her choice," as the chief turned and walked away.

Shana was now being protected by the wolves and, everywhere she went, the wolves followed. No one would go near Shana, but they talked about her behind her back.

They also told all sorts of rumors about her. The winter season was beginning, and Shana's stomach was showing very big now, but every time she went outside, she put on a heavy fur so that no one saw that she was pregnant. Shana kept her pregnancy hidden from everyone in the village. She still walked to the river to catch fish, all the while being escorted by the wolves; some of her old friends tried to visit her, but Shana refused to talk to them or be friends with them, because she knew they were only trying to find out why she had cut herself off from all the other villagers.

Many of Shana's old friends knew the story about how Rulan had raped Shana, or tried to rape her and then lied. All of Shana's old friends also knew that Rulan was a chronic liar. They also knew that Shana would not have sex with him, but they were afraid to speak up, because they didn't want the villagers to disassociate them as they had from Shana.

Shana told her father there was something strange about herself.

He asked her to explain. He asked her if she was ill. Shana told him no. She told him that, when Rulan was holding her down, while trying to rape her, she was out of breath from struggling with him, "so I used my last breath to scream, but the sound that came out of me was not a scream, it was a howl. And after I howled, the wolves showed up and rescued me in seconds. I am so proud of them, so I was wondering if there is more to my life than what you have told me. I'm hoping and praying that Bo and I are not brothers and sisters, because I have noticed how everyone is trying so hard to keep us apart."

Her father said, "No, Bo is not your brother." He smiled. "That is one thing I can guarantee you. But there is more to the story about you and Bo. I just recently found out the story behind you and Bo and why you both are so attracted to each other. But I have been sworn to secrecy. I have decided to let you and Bo live your lives the way you want. I can't tell you anything, but I will tell you the wolves are the answer. The wolves are trying to bring both of you together for a reason. Bo is special, you are special, and your baby will be special. When you decide to leave, I will not try to stop you. If you decide not to come back to the village, I will understand."

Shana went for a walk with her wolves down to the river. Shana went into the freezing cold river and she said, "Bo, where are you and why won't you come for me?" she asked, then started to cry. She left the freezing river. The wolves grabbed her hand in their mouths and tried to lead Shana in a southerly direction, but she stopped and said, "No, Bo must come to me." She pulled away from the wolves. The wolves again tugged on her clothes, but Shana refused to go, as she continued to cry. Shana walked home, and the wolves followed to protect her. Shana dropped down on one knee, feeling pain in her stomach, as she strained to get back up on her feet. She could feel the baby move.

"No, it is not time for you to come out, so please be still, and the baby stopped moving. Shana knew the time was not right, because she was only six months pregnant. Shana made her way home half frozen from being in the river. She arrived home and her father asked her what happened, and she told him, "I thought about ending the pregnancy." Her father helped her out of the wet clothes and gave her something hot to eat and told her how stupid it was to do something like that.

He told her how the village people already thought she slept around, "and now you want them to think you are crazy, too? They will find out you are pregnant. And that will only bring more problems; you will only have given the chief and Sunny a reason to try to take your baby, especially if they find out it's Bo's. Please think next time before you think about doing something stupid."

Shana apologized to her father and promised it would never happen again. She ate the hot food and put on some dry clothes went outside to pick some beans, and two of her old friends saw her and went to talk to her, so they could get the truth and stop all the rumors. One of the Indian girls told Shana how sorry she was about all the rumors and all her troubles, and she stepped forward to hug Shana. Before Shana could step away, they embraced, and the girl stepped away and said, "You lied, you did have sex with Rulan. No wonder you have stayed away from everyone. You're pregnant and you tried to hide it. How many lies are you going to continue to tell?"

"You don't understand," Shana said, but they said, "Understand what, that you are nothing but a whore? We don't ever want to see your face again."

Shana asked them not the tell anyone, but within hours, the boy and his parents were at Shana's father's tent asking him if their son could have Shana's hand in marriage. They wanted to be a part of the baby's life. The chief and Sunny arrived, and Shana told the boy and his parents that she didn't have sex with him. "I don't love him and I will not marry him," telling them to leave.

"And furthermore, this is not his baby. Rulan is a liar, and he lied about the whole thing from the beginning."

Shana's father said, "She will not marry this kid, because he has brought nothing but shame and problems to this whole situation. This boy has brought nothing but shame to Shana with his lies. I'm sure he can marry another girl and ruin her life with his lies and bad, filthy habits."

Sunny told Shana, "Once again, you have disappointed me."

Shana said, "No, you have disappointed me, because you have no faith."

Sunny slapped Shana's face and called her an ungrateful little bitch. As Shana held her face, the wolves rushed to attack Sunny, but Shana stopped them.

The chief said, "This is what I mean, those wolves are a threat to this village, and I want them gone as soon as possible.

"The wolves were only trying to protect me," Shana said. "You will pay in the end for all your misdeeds and the evil you have shown toward me. You people are evil, and I don't want anything else to do with any of you. Now please leave our tent and never come back; otherwise, I will have the wolves attack anyone who comes here."

Chapter 10

Shana Leaves the Village to Find Bo

Exile is among the cruelest of acts, for
It separates the heart from the body.

Shana 20

Shana was now close to her delivery date. She was having more and more stomach pains. She told her father it was almost time for the baby to be born. She told him, "I can't wait any longer for Bo to come and visit, and I don't want my baby to be born here in this village. I will have to go to Bo."

"I will go with you," her father replied. "It's a long trip."

Shana said, "No, I need you to stay here so no one will know I have disappeared, and please don't tell the chief and Sunny where I have gone, because Sunny will come after me. She will surely try to keep me from Bo."

Her father said, "Ok, I will cover for you. I want you to leave in the morning."

"I will leave tonight," Shana said. "The wolves will guide me through the darkness. The sooner I have this baby, the better I will feel. With that, Shana packed some clothes and extra food and, later that night; she set off on her journey on foot to visit Bo. She asked the wolves to lead her through the darkness to Bo, and they tugged on her hand as if to say, "Come on." Shana walked for two days in the snow, up through the mountains to find Bo. The trip was a difficult on foot. Shana's labor pains started again, but this time, they were stronger than before. She knew she couldn't continue the journey, because, this time, she started bleeding from between her legs and she was all alone with only the six wolves.

Shana looked two of the wolves in the eyes and said, "Go find Bo and bring him back. Please hurry." The wolves took off running as fast as they could. The other four wolves lay down next to Shana to keep her warm. They sensed Shana's pain. Bo was still at least three miles away, and it took the wolves thirty minutes to get to Bo's cabin with only a few stops for water.

Cheyenne was outside collecting eggs, when the wolves arrived, and the wolves started howling, and all the other wolves started frantically gathering around.

Bo and Jim Bo came out of the cabin.

"Something's wrong," Bo said. He ran up to the two wolves and kneeled down and looked them in the eyes.

Then Bo yelled, "Jim Bo, get the horse and the cart. It's Shana. She's hurt."

Cheyenne said, "Well, what did they tell you is wrong with her?"

"They don't know," Bo said. "All they keep saying is that she's hurt, lying down and in pain, and she needs help. She's only a short distance from here, because the wolves are not breathing hard from the run, so that means they didn't run far." Then Bo told Jim Bo, "I'm going on foot with the wolves, but I told them to spread out and leave a trail so you can follow in the cart. I'm leaving now. I will see you when you get there."

Cheyenne said, "Bo, please hurry and be careful."

Bo and the wolves took off running, and Jim Bo was leaving with the cart, when Cheyenne said, "Wait! I'm going too," and she dropped her eggs.

Jim Bo said, "No, you wait here, because we don't know what kind of problems we're going to run into."

"I don't care," Cheyenne said, "I'm going with you. That poor girl is all alone in the woods."

The wolves left a trail, just as Bo told them, so that Jim Bo could keep up at a slower pace in the cart.

The wolves sniffed the air along the way, as they ran through the forest. As they got closer, the wolves started howling and they ran right to Shana.

When Bo reached Shana, the wolves were still covering her from the cold air.

Bo grabbed Shana and called her name, and she opened her eyes and said, "Hi, you finally came. I tried to come to you but I couldn't make it."

Bo kissed her many times and told her, "I love you. I will never let you go again. I missed you so much; I was coming to visit you after the winter was over. I have missed you ever since the day you left."

Cheyenne and Jim Bo finally arrived with the other wolves, and all the wolves gathered around trying to keep Shana warm. Shana was sweating, and she was in a lot of pain. Bo was still kissing her. They lifted Shana up onto the cart, as Shana squeezed Cheyenne hand in pain, without saying a word.

Cheyenne said, "Is it true?" and Shana said it was, and Bo said, "Is what true? What's wrong with her?" and Cheyenne said, "Shana is with child."

Bo backed up in surprise, and Shana said, "No, Bo. It's not what you're thinking. Don't you remember when we made love?"

Bo said he did.

"Well, this is your baby, because I have not made love to any other man but you. You're going to hear all kind of lies from the village and your mother."

Bo said, "My mother is right here, and she doesn't tell lies."

"Not Cheyenne," Shana clarified. "I'm talking about your other mother, Sunny. There are rumors that I was raped and that I slept around, but I swear to you, none of it is true."

"I trust you," Bo said, "and if you say it is not true, then I believe you."

"My father, Sunny, Cheyenne, and Jim Bo have been keeping some kind of secret from us," Shana said, "and we need to know what it is. It has something to do with the wolves."

Bo turned to Cheyenne and Jim Bo. "Is this true what she is saying?"

They said, "Yes, but we will explain it all to you later. For now, we have to get Shana home, because I don't think your baby is going to wait."

Bo rode on the back of the cart with Shana and Cheyenne, while Jim Bo drove. Bo held Shana's hand, while she tried to fight the pain. Bo said, "I love you and I will marry you as soon as we are able to travel back to the village."

"Don't say things like that to me, unless you really mean it."

Bo said, "I mean every word of what I just said. But you should not have tried to come here all by yourself; you should have stayed at the village and had the baby there."

"I want to be with you," Shana said, and, as they rode in the cart, the wolves ran through the forest and along the ridgeline. They finally arrived home and they took Shana into the new log cabin.

Shana told Cheyenne, "I like your new cabin; it's beautiful."

Cheyenne thanked her, then she told Bo to boil some hot water, and Jim Bo brought some more blankets. They heard scratching at the door and it was Fang.

When Bo went to Shana she asked, "Where are my six wolves?"

Bo said, "You don't have any wolves."

"Yes I do, Shana said. "Open the door and let them in."

So Bo opened the door, but there were no wolves there.

Shana said, "Watch this…" and she let out a howl, and the six wolves ran into the log cabin. Bo stepped back.

Jim Bo and Cheyenne just looked at each other, and Cheyenne said, "The secret is out."

"These six wolves have been my guardians angels since you've been away," Shana said. "I returned home, and they saved me from being raped, and they have been guarding me ever since. I thought you sent them to protect me."

"I didn't," Bo said. "I don't know why they're protecting you. I will ask them why." Bo looked into one of the wolf's eyes and asked him, "Why are you protecting Shana?" and the wolf told Bo, "because she is my sister."

Bo told Shana what the wolf said. "That makes you just like me, so that makes you part wolf. How you became a part of the clan I don't know," Bo said, "But somebody has to know the answer. There are too many secrets going around, and we need to find out the truth." Bo looked at Jim Bo and Cheyenne and told them, "I want to know the whole truth."

"We will tell you everything we know after Shana has the baby," Cheyenne promised.

At that moment, Shana started screaming and said the baby was coming.

"Push!" Cheyenne said. "I can see the baby's head."

Shana kept pushing, and Cheyenne said, "Ok, here it comes; it's a little girl." Bo was smiling and happy, then Shana screamed again and called for Cheyenne.

"Something's wrong."

Cheyenne said, "What's wrong?"

Shana said, "I am having those pains again; something's wrong."

Cheyenne said, "Hold on, let me take another look." A moment later, she said, "Wow I hate to tell you this, but there is another baby down here."

Bo said, "Are you sure?"

"Yes," Cheyenne said. "I'm looking at a baby's head sticking out."

"I don't think I can do this again," Shana said.

"Don't do anything; just let it happen naturally. Don't even push. Just let the second baby come out on its own."

With a bit of fear, Shana asked Cheyenne, "Do you think there's a third one inside of me?"

"I don't know, but whatever's in there will come out."

Jim Bo just stood there holding the blanket.

Cheyenne said, "Ok, it's coming out, Shana, so don't push, and Shana didn't even scream. When the second baby came out, Cheyenne told her, "It's a boy."

Cheyenne told Bo, "You now have a little boy and a little girl." They wrapped both of the babies in blankets and gave them to Shana; Bo kissed Shana and told her, I will never let you go again. We will be together as a family."

"Shana, what are you going to name the babies?" Cheyenne asked.

Shana said, "I will name the boy Layto, and the girl will be Shion."

Jim Bo asked Cheyenne if the babies were blue and she replied, "No, and they both seem to be healthy."

Bo told his parents that he would stay in the room with Shana and the wolves and serve her every need.

Cheyenne just smiled and winked at Shana because she knew Shana had finally broken down the wall between Bo and the wolves. As she walked out of the room, Cheyenne told Bo and Shana good night.

Cheyenne went to wash up, and Jim Bo was in the other room with Fang. While Cheyenne was washing up, Jim Bo came up behind her and gave her a big hug. "You have raised a fine young man, and now you have a fine young daughter. You have gotten what you always wished for, and that is a son and a daughter. You are one lucky woman. I love you with all my heart," Jim Bo said.

"What about the grand babies?" Cheyenne asked Jim Bo. "Shana will be going back to the Indian village once she gets back on her feet."

"Did you see the look on Bo and Shana's faces?" Jim Bo asked. "I don't think she will ever go back to that village. All the lies and problems they put that poor girl through? If she ever goes back she would only go to visit her father."

Then Jim Bo told Cheyenne, "I might have to start building another log cabin for Bo and Shana and the children."

"Why can't they continue to live with us?" Cheyenne asked.

"We don't have enough room for all these wolves, plus these wolves can't be domesticated," he said. "They're wild animals, and they must stay outside. But since Bo and Shana love the wolves too much to put them outside, they will need their own cabin."

"If it will make you feel better, I will build it right next door; that way, you can always see your grandbabies and your son will always be near you."

Cheyenne kissed Jim Bo and they went to bed.

Then next morning, Bo told Cheyenne and Jim Bo that he wanted to marry Shana.

"There's no rush," Jim Bo said. "Wait until she gets better and gets her strength back."

Then Jim Bo turned to Shana. "Your father will be glad to see the babies."

"He will have to come here," she said. "I will never allow my babies to step foot in that village, and I will never let the chief or Sunny see them, after the way they treated me and shamed me and my father. I was not worthy to be their daughter or I was not good enough for their son, so that means my kids are not good enough for them, either. They don't even need to know I was ever pregnant with Bo's babies; my father is the only one that knew."

Cheyenne told Shana, "Ok, no more secrets; that is why we have this big mess now."

"Ok, no more secrets," Shana agreed. "But they still won't get near my babies, even if I have to have the wolves protect them. When I'm better, I will go to the village and have my father marry me and Bo. I will leave the babies here with you and Jim Bo, and the wolves will be here to guard them. I will tell my father to come out here to visit the babies whenever he wants. We will wait a few months before we get married, and then we will come straight back here. Is it ok if we live in your old tent? That way, we won't be in your way."

Cheyenne said, "You're welcome to live right here in the cabin with us, as long as you like; But Jim Bo had an idea to build you and Bo your own cabin next to ours."

"That will be great, and we will help you," Shana said.

Cheyenne told Bo and Shana, "Now that the babies are born, can we put all the wolves back outside?"

Jim Bo said, "No, Fang stays."

"Fang stays outside too," Cheyenne said.

Bo said, "It's ok, Fang. I will sleep outside with you."

Cheyenne laughed. "Ok, Fang can stay inside, but it's only because I don't want Bo sleeping outside. But tomorrow I want Jim Bo and Bo to start right away building Shana's new log cabin. Shana, are you sure you want to stay here permanently?"

"Yes," Shana said, "you are my new family."

Bo told Shana, "When you get better, we'll figure out the story about you and the wolves."

Shana said, "I have to feed the babies, so everyone get out of the room but Cheyenne. I need her to help me. I'll feed them one at a time, and hopefully, they will feed, so we won't have the same problem that Bo had."

Shana tried to breast-feed Shion, the baby girl, and she fed with no problem; after finishing, Shana tried feeding Layto, and he also fed with no problem.

Cheyenne reminded Shana not to expect too much because there was a chance the babies would be part wolf like herself and Bo.

Chapter 11

Bo Marries Shana

An obligation without honor is worthless

Bo 21

Jim Bo finally decided it was time to start building Bo and Shana's log cabin. Jim Bo asked Bo, "Are you ready to do some hard work, because I'm ready to build your new cabin."

"I'm ready when you are," Bo said. So they took the cart into the woods and started cutting down more trees. Bo had regained all of his strength after the grizzly bear attack.

Shana and Cheyenne were back at the cabin with the twins. Cheyenne was happy to have grandbabies. She was playing with both babies now as they crawled around on the floor. Shana was sewing some clothes for the babies to wear. Four months has passed and the babies was growing fast

Cheyenne asked Shana if Bo had decided what day he wanted to get married.

Shana replied, "He has left that up to me, but I want to wait until the babies get a little older, or at least until they are both walking."

Cheyenne said, "I could take care of them for you while you go and get married."

"Ok, but I still would like to wait until the babies get a little older."

"When you move into your new cabin," Cheyenne said, "will the wolves be living in there with you?"

"No, but we will allow them to continue to spend a lot of time with the babies."

"I don't care if they're around; there're just so many of them."

"Ok, I will ask Bo to speak to them; you know he loves those wolves."

"Yes, I know," Cheyenne replied. "We have to start getting dinner ready; when the men come home they will be ready to eat."

Shana said, "I'll have the wolves keep an eye on the babies while we get dinner ready." Shana waved her hand, and the wolves came over and lay down, and Shana laid both of the babies down with the wolves, and they went fast to sleep.

Cheyenne said, "It's amazing how the babies just attach themselves to the wolves like that. Bo was the same way when he was a baby. Were you like that?"

"I don't know, there were never any wolves around."

Bo and Jim Bo arrived with the logs and started to work on the new cabin. Cheyenne asked them both to stop and eat, and Jim Bo replied, "This cabin is not going to build itself."

Bo said, "Dad, we have time; let's eat first, and then we can start building again. So they sat down and ate dinner.

Shana asked Bo, "When are we going to get married?"

"After the cabin is built," he said.

Cheyenne told Bo, "You promised Shana you would marry her as soon as she got back on her feet, and she is still waiting. Make this year the last promise and take her to the village and marry her."

"I will, mother, I promise." Jim Bo and Bo finished eating and went back to building the house. They continued working until nightfall. Everyone went inside, and the wolves tried to enter, but Shana made them all stay outside, including Fang. The next morning, once again, Bo woke up early, stripped off all of his clothes, and walked outside with the wolves and started running; the wolves took off running behind him as he led the pack. They ran for miles, having fun; the wolves really enjoyed running with Bo. The wolves were getting hungry, but Bo refused to hunt with them, so on their way back home, Bo told them to continue and go hunting for food, and Bo ran back home with fang. Bo ran for miles and never got tired, but he decided to take a break and go to the river and wash off before going home. So he stopped at the river, and when he finished, he continued on home with Fang running beside him. When he arrived, Shana was upset because he had run off with the wolves. Bo didn't care, because he loved his wolves.

Jim Bo told Shana, "I know what you're thinking, but you need to let it go, before you put a wedge between you and Bo over those wolves."

Cheyenne told Shana, "I'm warning you, do not try to make Bo choose between you and the wolves, because you will lose and you might lose Bo, and that's a chance you don't want to take."

"But he never spends any time with the babies, because he spends all his time with those wolves."

Cheyenne said, "Please give him some time; he will change."

"Shana, have you ever thought about running with him?" Jim Bo asked. "You're part wolf, too, you know. You should try it, and don't worry about the babies; we will take care of them when you go running."

Shana turned to Bo. "The next time you go running with the wolves, can I go?"

"Yes, but we have to train you; otherwise, you won't be able to keep up, because when we run, we run far and wide. But don't worry; I'll train you. I'll teach you how to run, fight, and hunt with the pack. We'll start training in the morning. As Bo left to go back to work on the cabin, Shana walked past Jim Bo, and he smiled and winked at her.

"Shana, are you ready for this so soon after you have just had, not one, but two babies?" Cheyenne asked.

Shana said, "If I'm going to win Bo's heart, I want his whole heart, and I want to be with the wolves too, if I have to share him with them. The next day, Shana started her training. She and Bo exercised together, and she helped Bo and Jim Bo build the new log cabin, as Cheyenne and the wolves watched over the babies. Later on in the day, Bo taught Shana how to fight with her hands and feet. He taught her how to throw knives, and Jim Bo made her a boomerang. She practiced short distance running and hunting skills with Bo and the wolves.

After three months of training and work on the cabin, the new log cabin was now finished.

"Now for the big test," Bo told Shana. "We'll go for a long-distance run with the wolves, and you will lead the pack. You can go as far as you like and we'll follow."

Bo asked Cheyenne and Jim Bo if they would watch the babies, and Cheyenne said, "You don't ever have to ask."

Jim Bo said, "Go and good luck."

Shana grabbed her gear and took off running with little or nothing on at all.

Jim Bo asked Cheyenne, "Do they always have to run with no clothes on? They're not savages, you know."

Cheyenne just laughed and touched Jim Bo's stomach and said, "Maybe you should run with them," and he laughed.

"I'm too old. I wouldn't even make it past the tree line before I fell down trying to get some air."

As Shana ran through the forest, Bo realized she was in perfect shape. So he wondered how far she could run. And to his surprise, she ran for miles, and she even stopped and howled a few times, telling everyone to keep up. As Shana ran, Bo looked at her beautiful body and her long, silky, black hair. As Shana ran, she never got tired; it was as if she was born to run.

Bo finally realized Shana was a part of the wolf pack and she too was half wolf; she just needed someone to guide her to find out who she really was.

As Shana ran, she realized that she and Bo were destined to be together, and it was their destiny to run with the wolves.

Bo told Shana, "You have proven yourself; now we should turn back."

"I was not trying to prove myself," Shana replied. "I was just enjoying the run; so, how far did we go?"

"Over fifty miles," Bo replied, "and that is unusual. The wolves are tired, but we can make it back, so it's up to you to lead the way, but, before we go, I need to check something."

"What do you need to check?"

"Your teeth." So Shana opened her mouth, and Bo said, "Now feel your teeth, and Shana touched her teeth and she could feel the fangs in her mouth.

"You are truly a wolf. You're one of us. It was not you running; it was the wolf in you that was taking over. Once you stop and rest, you will return to normal. Ok, now let's go home. You lead the way and we will follow."

So Shana took off running again, and she even howled again to tell everyone to keep up, because she wasn't tired. She was so happy now to be a part of the wolf pack, and the wolves accepted her as another leader. The pack ran for hours, going home, stopping at the river to wash, and Shana and Bo both reverted back to their normal state, so his parents wouldn't see them in their wolf form.

Bo and Shana returned home and Jim Bo asked Bo and Shana, "How was your run?"

"Shana is part wolf, just like me."

"How do you know?" Cheyenne asked.

"She ran fifty miles there and fifty miles back. And no normal person can do that. She has fangs and she howls like a wolf. I am so proud of her, but I didn't expect her to be just like me. I trust her, and I believe all the things she said happened to her at the village. We will live next to you and dad. Tomorrow, we will start moving into our new log cabin, now that it's finished. It will give you and dad more room and more privacy for yourselves."

Jim Bo had secretly built furniture for Shana's new cabin. They all sat down for dinner and, after dinner, Bo and Shana went straight to bed because they were tired from the long run earlier in the day. While they were lying in bed, Bo rolled over and told Shana, "Let's take the horse in the morning and ride to the village and get married."

"Please don't joke like that," Shana said.

"I'm not joking. I love you with all my heart, and I want you to be my wife."

She smiled and kissed Bo and said, "Yes, I will marry you."

Bo said, "Ok, we will leave in the morning."

"What about the cabin? We're supposed to move in tomorrow morning."

"It can wait," Bo said. "We'll get married first and come right back and move in. I'm sure my mother will watch the twins for us."

When morning arrived, Shana told Cheyenne and Jim Bo the good news and they agreed to watch the babies.

Jim Bo said, "I hope you two are not planning on running to the village and back."

Bo said, "No, we'll ride my horse. We'll take Fang and all the wolves with us."

Bo and Shana saddled up the horse and rode to the village and, upon their arrival, everyone watched as they rode in on Bo's pretty white horse. All the girls were pointing at Bo, wishing they could have him. And some girls were jealous that he was Shana's. All the young men were surprised at how beautiful Shana had become in a short time, and she was very muscular from the training that Bo had taken her through. Bo and Shana rode to Shana's father's tent and, when he came out and looked up at Shana and Bo, he said, "It's about time you two showed up. I thought you had forgotten about the old man."

"No, father, I will never forget about you," Shana said.

He saw that it was only Shana and Bo, and said, "Oh no, please don't tell me the baby didn't make it."

Shana smiled. "The babies are fine."

"Babies?" the medicine man said. "You mean to tell me there is more than one?"

"A boy and a girl," Shana said, smiling. "Their names are Layto and Shion. You have to come and visit sometime and see them."

All the villagers arrived with the chief and Sunny.

Sunny saw Bo and ran to him and hugged him, and the chief walked up and greeted Bo and Shana. "Welcome to the village."

I hope everything is well," the chief said, "and I consider the problem we had with Shana and the rape accusation to be solved."

"Although we are not here for that," Shana said, "I don't consider the matter to be solved. Bo and I have come here to ask my father to marry us. We are also here to punish the both of you."

The chief said, "You can't punish me, young lady, I am the chief of this village."

"Well, Chief, I have the perfect weapon. That so-called attempted rape that you dismissed so easily, well it was the truth, and I never lied, and the reason the story didn't sound right is, I was already pregnant with Bo's babies."

Sunny said, "You mean to tell me I have two grand babies?"

"No, you don't have anything, "Shana said. "I forbid you to ever come near my twins, and I dare you to try. I have given the wolves strict orders to tear you or the chief apart if you ever go near them. That is your punishment for treating me the way you did." Rulan, the liar, walked up to Shana and, within a split second, her knife was at his throat. "You little lying bastard; all of this mess is your fault. I am now a trained warrior, and if you ever come near me again, I will kill you where you stand, myself."

"Shana, all this violence is not necessary," the chief said.

"Yes, chief, you are right, and I apologize for my bad behavior. I realize I don't belong here anymore, so once my father marries us, Bo and I we will leave. I will live with my husband and kids, among my brothers and sisters up in the mountains."

Sunny said, "Shana you don't have any brothers or sisters, so why are you trying so hard to be like Bo? You will never blend in; you belong here."

"No, that's where you are wrong, once again," Shana said. She got up close to Sunny and the chief and howled, and her fangs extended, and the wolves came out of the tree line.

Shana said, "Meet all my brothers and sisters. You see, I am one of them, too, and I have always been. I just didn't know it until the wolves and Bo showed me the way. And another thing, both of my twin babies, Layto the boy and Shion the girl, are half wolf too, so deal with it, because you will never see them."

Shana's father quickly gave them the wedding sermon and gave them a gift, and Shana and Bo climbed back up on his horse. Shana turned and said, "Father, you are always welcome to visit us anytime," and she waved her hand and all the wolves went back into the tree line. Shana and Bo rode away with Fang running beside them.

Chapter 12

Bo and Shana Live Happily Ever After

*A single journey of a thousand miles begins
with a single step.*

Doug Green

Bo and Shana returned home as husband and wife.

Cheyenne and Jim Bo were there to greet them with Layto and Shion. Both babies were happy to see their mother and father.

Shana told Bo, "Now that we are back, we can worry about building furniture for the cabin."

Jim Bo told Shana not to worry about that. "It has already been taken care of," he said with a smile. "The furniture is already in your cabin and you can move right in."

Shana and Bo thanked Jim Bo and Cheyenne for all their help. They went into their new cabin and walked around. Shana was happy that she had finally gotten everything she wanted.

Bo went outside and looked at the wolves and then he looked back at Shana and his twins. A deep feeling of sorrow came over him.

Bo told Shana he was going for a walk with the wolves, and Shana said she wanted to go with him; then she stopped and turned around, looking at Cheyenne holding both babies. She suddenly realized her place was there with her children. So, she told Bo, "Go ahead without me."

"I'll take the babies," Shana told Cheyenne. "You could spend some time with your husband."

"It's ok," Cheyenne replied. "I'll stay and help you attend to the babies," and she held one baby while Shana held the other one.

"I wish I could spend time with him and the wolves," Shana said "but I have to stay with the babies."

"Why, can't you take the babies with you?" Cheyenne asked. "I'm sure it will be just as much fun. You and Bo could take the babies down to the river with the wolves, and you could be one big happy family. I'm sure Bo would like to spend time with his family and the wolves."

Bo went down to the river with the wolves, but he wasn't happy without Shana and the twins. So he walked with the wolves a short distance and then went back home. When he arrived home, Shana asked him why he was back so soon.

Bo said, "It's not the same without you."

Shana told Bo, "Then maybe tomorrow, we could all go down to the river and spend some time together like a family."

Bo smiled, brightening. "I would like that a lot."

"I'll make dinner," Shana said, but Cheyenne said everyone could eat at her cabin. "You should be tired from the marriage and the long ride home from the village."

They all sat down to eat dinner, and Shana told Jim Bo and Cheyenne all about the wedding.

"My father was happy to learn that the twins were ok." She told Cheyenne how her father thought that there was only one baby and was surprised to learn there were twins.

She told everyone how he said he would come and visit soon.

Then Shana told Cheyenne and Jim Bo how she had told the chief and Sunny that they could never see the twins, as their punishment for treating her badly and accusing her of sleeping around and disrespecting her and allowing her to be the talk of the village.

"But, Shana, what if they try to come and visit anyway?" Cheyenne asked.

"They know if they come near the twins, the wolves have orders to attack them."

"But Sunny is their grandmother," Cheyenne said.

"No she is not," Shana said. "You are their grandmother; you even helped me birth them. I owe everything to you, Cheyenne. I will be forever in your debt for all you have done for me."

Then Shana turned to Jim Bo. "I have not forgotten you, Jim Bo. You have always gone out of your way to make me feel comfortable and feel at home, here. Both of you have accepted me with open arms, ever since the first day I met both of you. When I was sad, you always talked to me and cheered me up and, again, I am grateful for all your support."

After dinner, Bo and Shana took the twins and went into their cabin, followed by Fang.

Jim Bo and Cheyenne went into their cabin to the peace and quiet. There were no babies crying and no wolves howling.

Cheyenne and Jim Bo went to bed and just held each other.

Jim Bo said, "Wow, everything is finally back to normal."

Shana and Bo were so tired from their long trip that everyone went right to sleep. The next morning, Shana was up early exercising and practicing combat fighting moves. She practiced her knife fighting skills and knife throwing skills. She practiced throwing her boomerang. It didn't matter how far she threw, it always came back and landed right in her hand. She even thought of asking Jim Bo to design her a special boomerang with blades on the edge for cutting through things. She thought how nice it would be when the twins, Layto and Shion, got older, how she could teach them how to run, hunt, and exercise with her when they were not out running with the wolves. Shana continued to train outside. She wanted to be the first and only female warrior that was ever trained in the Indian tribe. She was already a better fighter than most of the men from her tribe.

Cheyenne finally came outside and talked to Shana while she trained. She asked Shana if she wanted her to get Layto and Shion, but she said, "No, I can handle being a warrior and a mother at the same time. I appreciate your help, but I'm beginning to learn how to handle things on my own. I still have a lot to learn, but I think I will be ok." Both of the babies crawled to the door and stood up and tried to walk, and Cheyenne ran to them, but Shana said, "Let me handle it. I have to start putting them first, so I will stop exercising for now and take care of them."

Cheyenne said, "But I've gotten attached to them, so Shana handed her Layto, admitting she could still use a little help.

"You can help me feed them while we talk," she said, and they both laugh and joked as they entered the cabin.

Bo was still asleep and Jim Bo was still asleep next door. They fed the babies as Shana cooked breakfast.

Jim Bo came to Shana's cabin and said, "So this is where everyone is hiding out." Then Bo finally woke up and Shana gave him his breakfast.

Bo told Shana he was going outside to exercise then he would eat breakfast. Bo went outside, and the wolves wanted him to go hunting, but Bo told them that he would come and visit them at the den later to play with the puppies. The wolves left without Bo and went hunting.

Bo started exercising and performing the same routine as Shana. After he finished training, he went back into the cabin to eat breakfast and played with Layto and Shion on the floor. He told Shana that, when the twins got older they could run with them and the wolves in the forest. "I'm sure the wolf pack would love that."

"We need to wait until they get a little bit older," Shana said. "Maybe when they reach the age of about ten or twelve years old. But before that, you can teach them how to hunt. You can even teach them how to throw knives and the boomerang."

Jim Bo said, "I will teach them how to fish," and Shana said, "Yes. Father and everyone were surprised, and Jim Bo felt good because now he had the daughter he had always wanted. Everyone was now happy, because all the pieces were falling into place. There were no more secrets, and everyone knew both Bo and Shana were half wolf, and they also knew the twins would be half wolf, too. Both the twins had normal colored skin, but everyone also knew they were half wolves, because the wolves still protected them. The wolves had been protective of them even when they were conceived; the wolves had apparently known they would be new members to the clan before Shana even realized she was pregnant. Shana always wondered why the wolves always followed her around. She thought maybe it was because they didn't trust her, but it was because they knew she was part of the wolf pack, even though they had never met her.

Bo told everyone, "Enough talking about the past; we need to start thinking about our future. From this day on, we will all be one happy family.

Later that day, Shana and Bo went to the wolves' den to check on the pups, and they told the wolves they had to stay near the den and live like wolves.

Bo told the wolves that he and Shana would visit them from time to time. They stayed at the wolves' den and played with the puppies. They lay down with the wolves and relaxed. After a few hours, Bo and Shana walked home, but they told the wolves to stay.

Shana told Bo how much she loved the wolves.

"There is a lot more I need to teach you," Bo said. "I need to teach you how to talk to the wolves; we will use Fang to help you." When they returned home, Shana went to Cheyenne's cabin where the twins were taking a nap, so Shana didn't wake them; she just sat down and talked to Cheyenne. They talked about the village chief and Sunny and why they had abandoned Bo when he was a newborn baby.

Cheyenne explained to Shana that Bo's abandonment had not been intentional and that Sunny was not a bad person. Cheyenne reminded Shana that if she cut Bo and the twins out of Sunny's life it would hurt her.

Shana told Cheyenne, "I'm not trying to cut Bo out of Sunny's life; that is up to Bo. But I will not let her or her husband near my son or daughter. They have a mean and nasty attitude, and I don't want my kids around them. I'm using my kids to punish them for how they treated me and how they tried to push me out of the village, until they found out the twins were Bo's; then they asked me to stay so they could be near the twins. When they thought I was sleeping around, they tried to label me as unclean. I tried to explain to them that the Indian boy tried to rape me, but they took his side of the story, because they are friends with his parents. I even tried to explain to them that the boy was a chronic liar, and they still didn't believe me. When they found out I was pregnant, they even tried to force me to marry that lying bastard.

"Rulan even told Sunny and the chief that the baby was his, even when he knew we never had sex. He never told them I used the wolves to make him apologize and beg for his life. I didn't want to tell the truth, because I didn't want to reveal that the wolves had protected me. I was afraid that they would have gone after the wolves to attack them and say the wolves were a danger to the people in the village.

"The wolves protected me, which is why I will never sacrifice them. I will protect them until the day I die. The wolves risked their lives to protect my family, so I will do whatever I can to protect them. I'm sure Bo feels the same way about protecting the wolves."

"But, Shana," Cheyenne said, "you are carrying a heavy burden; if you let these things go, you will feel a lot better."

Jim Bo and Bo told Shana and Cheyenne that they were going to the woods to try to catch some dinner, and they wanted to take the twins with them.

Both Shana and Cheyenne said they were too young.

Shana said, "Maybe you could take them with you in about five years."

Jim Bo said, "Ok, we'll be back in a little while." The twins were still asleep.

Cheyenne and Shana were talking, and Cheyenne said, "Don't look now, but you have a visitor."

Shana turned around and saw that a cougar was creeping up behind her. Shana said, "What should I do?"

"You need to accept her," Cheyenne said, as the cougar walked up and rubbed up against Shana; so she rubbed the cougar and gave her a hug. The big cougar climbed up in Shana's lap, and Shana accepted the cougar and continued to rub her while she and Cheyenne continued talking.

Cheyenne winked at Shana. "You have just made a new friend. You're doing a good job."

The cougar stayed a short while, then she stood up and gave Shana a hug, and Shana kissed the cougar and the cougar rubbed her face on Shana's face, and then she climbed down off of Shana's lap and slowly walked away. The cougar went back into the forest as Shana waved goodbye. The babies were now awake so Shana cared for Shion and Cheyenne cared for Layto.

Jim Bo and Bo returned from hunting, with a rabbit and a chicken to eat for dinner. Shana looked at Bo, but he pointed to Jim Bo and said, "It was his idea."

Cheyenne decided to prepare dinner for everyone, while Shana cared for the twins. Later, they ate dinner, and then everyone went home. Once the twins were put to bed, Shana and Bo went to bed. Shana and Bo were madly in love as they kissed, then they passionately made love before falling asleep in each other's arms.

The next morning, Bo and Shana woke up early and went outside to train and exercise together; after about an hour, the wolves started showing up for their daily run, and Shana said, "Bo, you can have the chance to lead the pack."

Bo told Shana, "We can't leave the twins all alone."

But just then, Cheyenne came out of her cabin and asked Shana, "Do you need me to watch the twins, while both of you go running through the forest?"

Cheyenne said, "Let me get the twins before both of you start stripping out of your clothes." She went into the cabin and picked up both babies and went back to her cabin.

Jim Bo asked Cheyenne where Shana and Bo were, and Cheyenne said, "They're outside stripping off all their clothes to go running with the wolves."

"Well, I should have known not to ask," Jim Bo said. He looked out of the window and saw Shana and Bo running happily through the forest with their wolves, howling.

Jim Bo walked away from the window and said, "Those kids are crazy, but as long as they are happy then I am happy."

* * *

In the future, if you ever visit the northern mountain region and you see two or four faint human figures in the distance running with a pack of wolves, it's probably Bo, Shana, Layto, and Shion.

The End

Made in the USA
Lexington, KY
18 May 2010